TIME HACKERS

LAYNE WALKER

Wild Mustangs Publishing, LLC

TIME HACKERS

This is a work of fiction.
All characters and incidents are a product
of the author's imagination.
Any relationship to persons living or dead
is purely coincidental.

ISBN-13: 978-0-9883534-4-2

Published by
Wild Mustangs Publishing, LLC
Lake Havasu City, AZ

Visit Layne's website at
laynewalkerbooks.com

Printing history
First edition published July 2013

DEDICATION

To Anne,
my one and only.

ACKNOWLEDGMENTS

Thanks to Anne Cote, for all her hard work getting this book ready to publish.

Thanks to Anita Batz for all the feedback.

Thanks to the members of the
Lake Havasu City Writers Group.
Your critiques helped make this story what it is.

And thanks to anyone else out there who let me bounce ideas off of them.

CHAPTER 1

WRAAAWOO, *wraaawoo, wraaawoo.*

Startled by the strange noise, sixteen-year-old Jeff Watson paused the video game he and his friend Mitch Arnoldson were playing. He glanced around his bedroom. The late morning sunlight filtered between the blinds and highlighted the scattered clothes carelessly thrown on the beige carpet. He didn't hear the noise again, so he shrugged it off and resumed the game.

Wraaawoo, wraaawoo, wraaawoo.

"What is *that*?" Mitch's deep bass voice sounded more curious than concerned.

"It's just my dork brothers screwing around." Irritated by the interruption, Jeff knew he should go check on them, but he hadn't been this far in the game, ever, and he didn't want to ruin his streak of good luck. Living in Lake Havasu, Arizona, he'd looked forward to this spring break to do whatever he'd wanted, but this year, his parents had expected him to watch his younger brothers. His dad had told him it would help him be more responsible. *Yeah, right.* Jeff didn't care what his brothers did, as long as they stayed in their room and left him alone.

Mitch set his game controller down. "I don't know, dude, that sounded like some kind of animal." He walked to the wall separating the bedrooms. Pushing his shoulder-length blond hair from his ear, he pressed the side of his face against the wall.

Wraaawoo, wraaawoo, wraaawoo. Thump, thump.

Mitch's blue eyes widened. "What the hell is that?"

Jeff threw the game controller down in frustration. "It's

probably just the T.V.," he mumbled. "I'll be right back." Tubular skylights in the ceiling directed the sunlight into the house, making the hallway so bright it hurt Jeff's eyes. His sock's slid on the slippery hardwood floor as he stomped down the brightly lit hallway to the bedroom that Riley and Wayne shared. "Listen, you little twerps," he said as he threw open the door.

The room was dark with the blinds down, curtains closed, and lights off. Highlighted in the shaft of light coming in through the now open doorway, Riley's laptop computer lay open in the middle of the floor with its screen black.

Jeff wondered why the computer wasn't on the desk where it belonged. He'd expected to see the boys wrestling on the floor or jumping on one of the twin beds. Instead, the room looked empty. He squinted into the dim recesses for his two errant siblings.

From his left, something about the size of a pig shot out of the dark and slammed into Jeff's legs. Jeff stumbled and almost fell. He grasped the door handle and managed to hold himself upright.

"Don't let it get away," ten-year-old Wayne yelled franticly as he made a dive out of the darkness for the creature's legs. He missed by a fraction of an inch.

"Wraaawoo, Wraaawoo," the creature squealed as it forced its way past Jeff.

Shocked, Jeff pushed the door open all the way and jumped away from it.

Riley, the klutzy twelve-year-old of the family, dashed after it. He tripped on Wayne's legs and ended up sprawled on the floor next to Wayne. His glasses, knocked loose when he'd hit the floor, hung off one ear. "Catch it," he shouted. "Don't let it get away."

Jeff momentarily froze in place, wondering what the hell was going on.

"Holy crap," Mitch yelled from the other bedroom.

Oh, oh, Jeff thought as he ran to his room, *if something gets broken, I'm gonna get blamed. Mom and Dad will punish me instead of my two bratty brothers.* He came to a sliding stop in his bedroom doorway.

Mitch, standing in the middle of the room with his back to Jeff, held Jeff's bedspread up like a matador's cape. His tall, well-muscled body swayed slowly from side to side. As Jeff opened his mouth to speak, Mitch lunged forward and dove headfirst onto the floor. "Ah, ha, I caught ya," he called out triumphantly. His muscles bulged as he wrapped his arms around the animal, thrashing violently under the blanket. Mitch wound his legs around the animal in an attempt to get it under control.

The creature squealed louder now, loud enough that Jeff worried the neighbors would hear it and come to investigate.

Mitch, with jaw clenched and blue eyes blazing, grunted and wrapped his long arms and legs tighter around the struggling thing. His determination to win the battle showed in the strain on his face.

"Good, you caught it," said Riley, obviously relieved. He pushed his way past Jeff to stand over Mitch. His mussed brown hair and torn shirt appeared to be the only casualties of his scuffle with the creature.

Angrily, Jeff stepped forward and grabbed his arm. "The question is, you little twerp, what is it and why is it here? You know Mom and Dad don't allow animals in the house."

"Don't worry," Riley said as he wriggled out of Jeff's grasp, "I'll make sure it's out of the house before they get home from work."

"Yeah, don't worry about it, bro," Wayne said, casually walking into the room and shutting the door behind him. Excitement glittered in his brown eyes. "We'll take care of it." A wannabe gangster this week, Wayne wore a white tank top, big baggy pants that hung halfway off his scrawny butt, and black-and-white tennis shoes. A baseball cap, its bill turned to the back, covered his unruly brown hair.

What a dweeb, Jeff thought as he watched Wayne walk next to Riley.

The thing under the blanket made a squealing noise similar to someone scraping fingernails down a blackboard.

Jeff cringed.

"Keep your voices down," Mitch said quietly. "If this thing's like most animals, covering its head should calm it down."

Riley knelt next to Mitch. He whispered, "Can you carry it to my room?"

"I heard that," Jeff said loudly, causing the thing to start squirming again.

Mitch gave Jeff a dirty look. He shook his head at Riley. "No, I can't carry him to your room, at least not until he's calmed down more."

Lowering his voice, Jeff said, "So, while that *thing* is calming down, why don't you tell us what it is and where you got it?"

A what-now? look passed between Riley and Wayne.

"It's a…science experiment for school," Wayne quickly said.

Jeff clenched his fists and fought to stay calm. "That doesn't tell me *what* it is."

"It's a cross between a dog and a pig," Riley stated as he stood up then plopped down on the bed. "Some kind of genetic mutation."

"Quit lying to me." Jeff crossed his arms over his tattered t-shirt and glared at his brothers. "This isn't some school project, so cut the crap and tell me what it really is and how you got it in the house."

Riley fumbled guiltily with his glasses, while Wayne looked to Riley to come up with the answer.

As Jeff waited, he worried what would happen when their mom got home. It was Friday and she was coming home early from work to get ready for the trip she and Dad were taking this weekend to Las Vegas. Having an animal in the house was going to throw her into a tizzy-fit. He had to get rid of it. Right now, from what he could figure with his two tight-lipped brothers, his best option was to play the co-conspirator to loosen their tongues. "If you don't tell me the truth, I can't help you hide it from Mom."

Riley jumped up with panic in his brown eyes. "Jeff, please, whatever you do, don't tell Mom."

Jeff had never seen Riley so shaken, but fortunately, he now had him right where he wanted him. "I promise I won't tell her, but you have to tell me what it is and where you got it."

"Okay." Riley hesitated for a moment and glanced at Wayne. "It's a baby…"

"*No*," shouted Wayne, grabbing Riley's arm. "You can't tell him. You know what will happen if you do."

Riley put his hands on Wayne's bony shoulders. "We have to. We don't have a choice. Who would you rather have find out about it…him or Mom and Dad?"

Wayne looked from Riley to Jeff and back again. With resignation on his face, Wayne dejectedly said, "Yeah, go ahead and tell him."

"So, what is it?" Jeff asked again.

"I'll be damned," Mitch exclaimed in awe. He had set the thing down and was looking under the bedspread.

Wondering why he hadn't thought to do that in the first place, Jeff stepped next to Mitch, knelt down, and peered under the cover. Plenty of light came in through the window for Jeff to see the animal, but it took a moment for him to register what he was seeing. He gasped in astonishment and shoved himself backward, landing on his butt.

Laughing, Mitch moved to the side.

From under the bedspread, a baby dinosaur peered out at Jeff.

CHAPTER 2

SYDNEY Terrance Davis, "Terry" to his co-workers, sat back in his chair in Washington, DC, and tapped the end of his pencil against his lower lip as he stared at his computer screen. The clock read 2:30.

The evidence was right there in front of him: the kid had traveled through time. At least, that's what his computer told him. Terry had linked his computer to the kid's so that whenever the kid accessed a certain program named "Time Hackers*,*" Terry's computer beeped.

The kid's name was Riley Watson, a twelve-year-old boy from Arizona who'd hacked into DARPA's computers eleven months earlier. Terry's supervisors had confiscated Riley's computer and had given it to Terry to search for any sensitive information Riley might have accessed. Terry spent several days figuring out the virtual path the kid had taken once he'd gotten into DARPA's restricted areas. Luckily, most of the files the kid had explored weren't very important, but one trail linked directly to Terry's department. He was in charge of a highly secret program called *Dark Wave*, a program that dealt with time travel. It looked like the kid had managed to hack past Terry's firewalls and get into some of his files.

Fortunately for Terry, he'd kept all his important files on a computer with no links to the internet. Being a hacker himself, Terry knew how easy it was to break into almost any computer, and he didn't want anyone to get to his private files.

Two months after receiving Riley's computer, Terry had struggled to open the folder called "Time Travel" on the kid's computer.

Now, his mind wandered back to that frustrating day he'd practically given up. Until then, he'd tried every trick in the trade to decipher the password and, still, he couldn't get the folder open. Envious that a twelve-year-old kid could come up with a password so hard to break, he'd picked up his mouse and slammed it down hard enough to crack the plastic housing. Knowing he could requisition another mouse, he slammed it down two more times. Ripping the cord out of the USB port, he threw the mouse into the trashcan.

He shoved his chair away from his desk and ran both hands through his kinky black hair. *Take a break. Get a snack. Let your mind work on the problem subconsciously.* Nodding to himself, he rose to his feet and stretched.

At six-foot-two and weighing two-hundred-and-fifteen pounds, Terry knew he didn't look like the average computer nerd. "Tall, black, and handsome," the ladies called him. It was true he had the body and good looks of a model, but a physical disorder in his muscles created an emotional state that overshadowed all his handsome features. The expression "froze like a deer in the headlights" fit him perfectly when he encountered uncomfortable situations.

Terry had been born with a condition that most people associated with goats...fainting goats. These poor creatures were afflicted with a rare genetic disorder in the muscles called *Congenital Myotonia*. When startled or scared, the goats would stiffen up and sometimes fall over, earning them the name of "fainting goats."

Although Terry's condition wasn't serious—he didn't faint when he was startled—he did freeze up for five or ten seconds when he was nervous, scared, or caught off-guard. It embarrassed him, to say the least. When women especially walked up to him, smiled at him, or simply looked at him, he stiffened up like a wax replica of Frankenstein in Madame Tussauds Wax Museum.

He'd been teased about this condition most of his thirty-three years. Middle school had been particularly traumatic. As a result, he'd become an introvert. He had no friends and no social life and no hope for either. Unless...

His one hope—the reason he spent so much time at

work—was to uncover the mysteries of time travel. He knew, without a doubt, his condition would be curable in the future, and he would do anything to travel forward in time and be cured. Not surprisingly, *Dark Wave* had become more than a job. It had become his obsession.

True, there were medications he could take that would minimize his muscle spasms so his episodes weren't quite so bad, but the side effects produced worse reactions than freezing up. Plus, he couldn't justify taking a medication that wouldn't completely stop his spasms. He found it just as distressing to freeze up for two or three seconds as it was to freeze up for five or ten seconds. It still made him look and feel like a complete idiot.

He didn't know why, but he sensed this Riley kid was on to something with the "Time Travel" folder. Sure, it sounded ridiculous that a kid that young could solve a problem as complex as time travel, but, hey, kids nowadays were more computer literate and smarter than ever before. Hell, at this very minute, instructors were teaching things in high school that Terry hadn't learned until his third year of college. It wouldn't surprise him if this new generation of techno wizards solved not only the secrets of time travel, but also the secrets of inter-planetary travel, perpetual motion, and how to power vehicles with ordinary household garbage.

Taking a break from his discouragement at the computer, Terry opened his office door about an inch and peeked into the hallway. Not seeing anyone, he pulled the door open and stuck his head out. The hall was empty. Hoping he wouldn't run into any one, he quickly walked to the vending machines at the end of the hall. Two minutes later, he returned to his office with a Snickers candy bar, a bag of Doritos, and a can of Diet Coke.

He sat down and opened his drink. Taking a sip, a new idea about the password came to him. *What if I...?* Putting his drink aside, he limbered up his fingers and hunched over the keyboard on a new quest to get into Riley's folder.

STARTLED by a knock on his door, Terry froze for five seconds. The reveries of the past faded away, replaced with the here and now and a brief recall that he had gotten a beep from Riley's computer activity. He had to get back to that, but for now, he stood up and peered through the mini-blinds covering the window on his door.

Sheila, his boss's secretary and the girl of Terry's dreams, stared back at him.

He almost froze again but he quickly looked away. His heart beat faster. His hands got clammy. He felt his face grow bright red. Fumbling with the knob, he cracked the door open just far enough to stick out his head. "Yes?" He cast his eyes down at her red high heels but couldn't help taking a couple of quick glances at her face and body.

"Hi, Terry. Mr. Clemmons wants to see you in his office." She smiled, showing her straight, perfectly white teeth. "You're late for your meeting. I tried to buzz you, but apparently you've got your phone off-line again."

The meeting. He'd completely forgotten about it.

Before he could formulate an answer, Sheila turned and sauntered down the hall, her shoulder-length blond hair bouncing with each step.

He couldn't help watching her slim hips sway seductively from side to side. Terry didn't know for certain, but he swore she swayed more when she knew he was watching her.

"You'd better hurry," she called over her shoulder. "Mr Clemmons is waiting and he doesn't have all day."

Upset about forgetting the meeting, Terry shut down his computer, grabbed a folder off his desk, and hurried out of the room.

CHAPTER 3

AS Jeff slowly got to his feet, he studied the animal. *This can't really be a dinosaur. Or is it? It sure looks like one. In fact, it looks just like a miniature version of a Triceratops I saw in a movie.* Bristle-type hair covered its mottled, greenish-brown skin. A bony frill circled its neck. Two small bumps—that Jeff assumed would later grow into horns—protruded above each eye. A third horn, two inches long, erupted from the nose above a narrow, horny beak. A thick stubby tail stuck out the back.

The dinosaur, if that's what it really was, had calmed down and seemed content to sit and stare at them. It had apparently decided they weren't going to hurt it. In fact, it seemed to be almost as curious about them as they were about it.

His mind in turmoil, Jeff turned and caught his reflection in the mirror hanging on the back of his door. His confused brown eyes stared back at him from his tanned face. As he turned away, he ran his hand across his brown buzz-cut and wondered what to do next. First and foremost, he had to figure out a way to get that creature…dinosaur…whatever it was…out of the house before his mom got home.

He glanced at the alarm clock sitting on his nightstand. *Eleven-forty already. Wow, I lost track of time.* His mom had told him she had meetings all morning from eight until two. He turned to his brothers and said menacingly, "Okay, you two, time to own up. What is this thing and where did you get it?"

Riley and Wayne looked at each other sheepishly.

"You tell him," Wayne said, elbowing Riley in the side.

"It was your idea."

"Well, you see, I kind of made a time machine out of an old laptop and we decided to go back to the Jurassic–"

"Yeah, right." Jeff rolled his eyes in disbelief. He turned to Mitch and held his palms up out to his sides. "Can you believe these two? They really expect us to believe they traveled millions of years into the past and brought home a new pet."

"No," Riley jumped in, "it was an accident. We didn't mean to bring him back with us." He twisted the tail of his shirt in his hands as he talked, a nervous habit he had when he was anxious or upset.

Coming to his defense, Wayne said, "That's true. It ran out of the bushes just as we were coming home. By the time we realized what was going on, it was too late to do anything."

"Oh, gross," Mitch said, pinching his nostrils and moving quickly away from the dinosaur.

A pungent odor assaulted Jeff's nose. He looked down. A pile of green goo with bits of leaves and stems of plants sat on the floor. "Great, the thing just took a crap on my carpet."

Wayne took his hat off and waved it in front of his face to clear the air.

Jeff hurried to open a window, letting fresh air into the room. "Wayne, go get something to clean up this mess. Bring back some air freshener, too. And shut the door when you leave." The last thing he needed was for the creature to get out of his room and run around the house.

Wayne slapped his hat on his head. "You got it, Homey." He opened the door, scurried into the hallway, and slammed the door shut.

"So," Mitch asked Riley, "what are you two dudes going to do with it?"

"We were going to take it back, but we couldn't catch it." Still looking guilty, Riley took off his glasses and cleaned them on his shirttail.

Jeff stayed by the window and held his hand over his nose. "You don't really believe them, Mitch, do you?" he asked in astonishment, keeping his eye on the animal and wondering where his brothers could have possibly picked up such a creature. He'd never seen anything like it in any pet store.

"It's kind of hard not to believe them," Mitch replied casually. "I mean, look at this thing, dude." He pointed to the animal, which watched them as if it understood that they were talking about it. "What else could it be? Not only that, you know what a genius Riley is with computers. Remember last year when he hacked into that government website and–"

Jeff huffed, cutting him off. "How could I forget? We had people from the FBI, CIA, ATF, HLS, and every other three-letter agency dropping by here for weeks. My parents are still angry about it." He looked hard at his brainy little five-foot brother. "But a time machine? You've got to admit, that's hard to believe."

Mitch shrugged. "I know, but how else can you explain this cute little thing?" He leaned forward to touch the dinosaur.

The animal growled and snapped at Mitch's fingers with its wicked-looking beak as Mitch yanked back his hand.

Wayne returned, carrying a roll of paper towels, two pairs of yellow rubber gloves, a garbage bag, miscellaneous cleaning fluids, and a can of air freshener.

Jeff grabbed the air freshener and generously sprayed it around the room. The flowery scent didn't eliminate the sour smell completely, but it helped to cover it up.

Riley moved to stand in front of Jeff. He tilted his head back to look up at Jeff, who stood eight inches taller. "I swear, I'm telling you the truth. You know how good I am with computers. All I did was take the–"

"Stop right there. I don't care how you did it. All I care about is getting this thing out of the house before Mom comes home. She will totally freak if she sees this...this...*thing* sitting in the house." He glared at both his brothers. "As usual, I have to fix your screw-ups or I'll get in trouble, too."

"No you don't," replied Wayne pulling on the gloves. "We can take it back home."

"Yeah, we'll take care of it," Riley said as he hesitantly took the second pair of rubber gloves Wayne held out to him.

"Why don't we all go?" Mitch asked eagerly. "We can

take a picnic and make a day of it."

From the first day of kindergarten, Jeff and Mitch had been best friends. Now, over ten years later, Jeff lashed out at him for being so contrary. "Shut up, Mitch. You're not helping. And stop encouraging them. You know as well as I do, they're lying. There's no way Riley made a time machine. It's impossible. This thing must have come from some exotic pet store or one of Riley's nerdy friends. We've got to get rid of it before Mom gets home."

"I'm not totally convinced that it's from the past," Mitch said, glancing at Riley and Wayne, "but can you think of a better way for them to prove it to us than by taking us back in time with them?"

Irritated, Jeff watched his brothers tearing off paper towels and picking at the foul clump lying on his carpet. He had no idea how they had managed to get the creature into the house while he'd been playing the video game. Maybe it did look like a dinosaur, but he was sure it could not have come from millions of years in the past. No matter what Riley claimed, there was no way he could have made a working time machine. "Tell me, right now, Riley," Jeff demanded, "where did you get that thing?"

Riley scrunched up his nose at the odor as he wiped up the mess and scrubbed the carpet. "I told you…the Jurassic era."

Jeff threw his hands in the air. "I don't believe this."

"Come on, dude," Mitch coaxed, "give them a chance to make things right. Let them prove it." Mitch had always had a special bond with Riley. He would go along with anything Riley wanted to do.

Jeff rolled his eyes in disgust. He looked at the clock. It was already noon. They were wasting time. Mom would be home in two hours. He decided to play along and let the little twerps fail at proving their claim at having a time machine, then he'd have to get the creature out of the house and hide it until they could figure out what to do with it. The pet store was too far away. Mom would never let him use the car without a good explanation or wanting to go along. Maybe one of Riley's friends would be willing to keep it.

Wayne stood up and studied the damp, light-greenish area

on the carpet. Apparently, he felt satisfied it was cleaned up enough because he nodded to himself and stayed on his feet.

"Okay, fine," Jeff blurted angrily, "let's go. Riley, go get your laptop so we can take this little guy home."

As Riley and Wayne quickly stripped off their gloves and threw them in the garbage bag with the pile of green goo and half the roll of paper towels, Jeff heard a car pull into the driveway. He hurried to the window. Fear shot through him. "Great, Mom just got home early."

CHAPTER 4

TERRY watched as his boss, Jake Clemmons, wrote a note on the report Terry had written up. Jake's bald head reflected the glow from the overhead florescent light recessed in the ceiling above his desk. *If his head was any shinier, I could use it as a mirror.* Terry suppressed a smile at the thought. He fantasized making Mr. Clemmons bow down to him so that Terry could check his own appearance and make sure he didn't have any food stuck in his teeth. *The jerk thinks he's so high and mighty. It would serve him right to be my personal mirror. Then, Sheila would look at me differently, not like I'm some kind of freak. I bet she–*

"Well, I guess that about covers it, Terry," Mr. Clemmons said, pushing the paper across the desk. "Make sure you get me a copy of the final report by this afternoon, okay?" He picked up the phone and started punching numbers.

Formally dismissed, Terry took the paper, mumbled a quiet goodbye, and made his way to the door. His thoughts turned to the dreaded trip back to his office through the hallways.

While Mr. Clemmons' office sat on the third floor of the three-story building, Terry's office was located on the first floor. He would have to make his way past other employees to get to his place of safety.

Glancing sideways at Sheila as he passed her desk, he almost froze when she gave him a little wave goodbye.

He turned into the hallway with his head down, sliding his shoulder along the wall so other people would have plenty of room to pass and he wouldn't have to get too close or make eye contact. He passed the elevator, preferring to take the stairs instead. He told himself that he needed the exercise, but in truth, he took the stairs to avoid other employees, most of whom used the elevator. The worst part of the trip would be going from the doorway of the first-floor stairwell to his office, which sat halfway down the hall.

As bad luck would have it, today two men and a woman stood at the vending machines located just outside the door of the stairwell. Terry cringed when he saw them through the small window in the door. He recognized the large, loud man as Mark. He hated running into Mark because the fiend always cracked jokes about Terry's disease.

Terry debated whether or not to wait until the three of them left or just hurry past and hope they wouldn't notice him. When he heard someone coming down the stairs from above, he had no choice. He would rather take his chance walking past the three people at the vending machine than to get caught cowering under the stairs like a scared puppy.

Damn, why do I have to deal with these people today? he thought as he threw open the door. Holding the report in his hands, he stared at it as though totally engrossed. Out of the corner of his eye, he saw Mark smile. *Oh, crap, here we go again.*

"Hey, Pops, how's it going?" Mark blared. Mark stiffened and shook his body like Terry did when he was having one of his attacks.

The other man laughed. "Good one, Mark."

"I don't get it," the woman said. "He's younger than you, so why do you call him Pops?"

"It's short for popsicle," Mark stated. "Because he's cold as ice and always freezing. Watch."

Though Terry had started down the hallway away from the harassers, he dreaded what was coming.

Mark took two long strides, grabbed Terry's arm, spun him around, and shouted, "*Boo!*"

Against his will, Terry froze in place.

"Oh, that's so mean," the woman said. She raised a hand to her face to conceal a giggle.

"It's okay, it doesn't hurt him. Plus, I think he kind of likes it. Don'tcha, Pops?"

Regaining control of his body, Terry turned and hurried down the hall. His mind filled with insults he wanted to throw at Mark, but he said nothing. He knew from experience it was better to keep his mouth shut. He couldn't win a shouting match when he kept freezing in place. It only served to give his opponent more time to think up better insults.

Safely back in his office, Terry leaned against the door. Relief flooded through him as the tension drained from his muscles.

"**OH,** oh," Wayne said. "Mom's home."

Riley's eyes got big.

"Quick," Jeff said. "Go to your room and act like nothing's wrong. Watch T.V. or something."

"How are you going to hide that?" Riley pointed to the dinosaur now sniffing the air as if it were checking out its new surroundings.

"By not letting her come in my room. Mitch, you stay here and keep an eye on that thing. Make sure you keep it quiet. I'll go talk to Mom and keep her from coming up here."

Riley cast a worried glance over his shoulder as he and Wayne hurried off to their room.

Mitch casually settled on the bed and resumed playing the video game.

"Don't get so involved in the game you forget to watch our visitor," Jeff said as he started to close the bedroom door.

"I got it, dude," Mitch called out.

Jeff hoped Mitch did have it. If not, the creature might make noise or get out of the room and wander downstairs. His pulse raced at the thought of his mom turning around and seeing the strange creature standing in the middle of the formal sitting room. She would freak out, *big time*.

He walked into the kitchen just as his mom entered from the garage. Already, four sacks of food sat on the island counter.

"Oh, good," she said brightly, her blue eyes beaming, "you can help me bring in the rest of the groceries." She set two gallons of milk on the table. On her way out to the garage again, she turned and looked at him. "Are you okay? You look a little…flustered or something."

"I'm just surprised to see you," he said, hoping his voice wouldn't crack under the pressure of lying through his teeth. He followed her out the door. "I didn't expect you home so soon."

"My afternoon appointments canceled, so I thought I'd get some shopping done." She popped open the trunk of the car. "I wouldn't have fun in Vegas knowing my boys didn't have anything in the house to eat."

Wow, that's an understatement. There's enough food here to last us a month, even if Mitch eats with us every day. Jeff started grabbing bags.

"What was that?" his mom said, looking up and cocking an ear. She turned her head from side to side, as if trying to hear a sound again.

"What? I didn't hear anything." Jeff listened carefully, worried that the baby dinosaur might begin screeching any moment.

"It sounded like an animal of some kind."

"It's probably the boys watching T.V. or Mitch playing a video game." *I really hope Mitch doesn't let that thing out of my room. If he does, I'm dead meat.*

"I'm sure that's it," she said as she grabbed two more bags from the trunk and headed for the house. "You boys know better than to bring animals into the house, don't you?"

"Of course, we do. You've told us about a gazillion times."

"If I've told you once, I've told you a *thousand* times. Don't exaggerate. It's just another form of lying."

"Yes, Mom," he said as he set the bags on the counter and headed back to the garage to get the rest of them.

As he went out the door, he expected her to be right behind him, Instead, he heard her say, "You finish bringing the groceries in. I'm going to gather up a load of laundry and get it started. I'll say hi to Mitch while I'm up there."

Jeff's heart raced. *Now what?* He couldn't tell her not to go in his room or she'd know for sure something was going on. His only hope was to keep her downstairs.

"Why don't you start putting the food away," he said in a

casual tone. "I'll go up and get my clothes so you don't have to walk up the stairs. I'm sure you're tired after being at work all morning."

Instead of being pleased by his thoughtfulness, she turned suspicious. "Why don't you want me to go upstairs?" She stared hard at him. "You kids aren't doing anything you aren't supposed to be doing, are you?"

"No . . . really we aren't. It's just that you and Dad are always telling me I need to help out around here more. So I am." He hoped she'd believe him. "In fact, why don't you show me how to do a load of laundry. Maybe I can start doing my own." He cringed at the thought of having to do the laundry regularly. *I'm getting myself in pretty deep here. I hope Riley and Wayne appreciate this.*

His mom laughed. "I don't think so sweetheart, but thanks for offering. I don't need you ruining our clothes while I'm gone this weekend. Maybe when your dad and I get back I can work with you on that."

Wraaawoo, wraaawoo, wraaawoo.

Jeff cringed. *Oh, no, Mitch, what are you doing up there? You're supposed to be helping me here.*

"Run upstairs and tell your brothers to turn down their T.V. They know better than to have it that loud."

"Sure, Mom." He started out of the room.

"Then come back and help me put this food away."

Yes, he thought as he rushed up the stairs. *Anything to keep you down here and away from my room and that animal.*

CHAPTER 5

OVER an hour later, Terry sat in his office chair and worked at his computer on his report for Clemmons. There had been no new activity on Riley's computer. After hacking into Riley's computer the first time, Terry now felt nervous that Riley would somehow detect his presence and lock him out. He wasn't sure he'd be able to get back in if that happened.

Terry sat back and thought about the two full months it had taken him to break the code to get into Riley's files. It had taken so long because Riley had cleverly used symbols, rather than letters and numbers, for his password. To make matters worse, the symbols weren't common symbols used in computer languages and fonts. Riley had invented them.

During those months, Terry had used every ploy possible to decipher the password. He thought out of the box. He gleaned information off internet forums about hacking. In the end, it was by a stroke of luck that he found the symbols at all.

Studying pictures Riley had created on his computer, Terry realized some of the pictures were made from keyboard art, using numbers, letters, and symbols. On one forum, Terry found a post about hiding a symbol-based password in one of these pictures. It made sense, especially since the symbols Riley used weren't readily available, and he couldn't just type them into the password box. For Riley to obtain the password, he had to copy them off one of the pictures and paste them into the box.

Feeling like he was on to something, Terry searched for a program that would decipher passwords hidden in keyboard-art pictures. To his glee, one of the programs worked, and he finally opened Riley's "Time Travel" folder to find two sub-folders and a software program. One folder named "Jurassic" only contained general information about the Jurassic era and dinosaurs that had lived during that era. The second folder contained a schematic showing how to wire an ordinary digital alarm clock, a handheld GPS, and an old cell phone into a laptop computer, along with five typed pages of information. Leaving the more detailed inspection for later, Terry opened the program called "Time Hackers." To his surprise, it presented boxes for the user to type in a GPS location and a date.

That's it?

Terry read and re-read the pages. He couldn't believe it at first, but on his third reading, he started to wonder if it could be true that Riley, a twelve-year old boy, really had invented a working time machine. His gut instinct told him to replicate Riley's work. He copied the folder to his computer and began experimenting with it.

It hadn't taken Terry long to cobble together the components and take his first trip through time. The first time he went back five minutes. The second time, he went back two months. The third, he'd not only gone back two years, he'd changed locations, too. Now that he knew all this was possible, he spent many hours figuring out what he wanted to do with the information.

Technically, he was supposed to report everything he discovered to Mr. Clemmons, but Terry knew if he did, he'd never be able to make and use a time machine for himself. Nobody, not Mr. Clemmons, not the head of DARPA, not even the President of the United States, would keep Terry from traveling into the future and curing his disease. No, he would keep all this a secret until he could find the right place and time to get the cure. In the meantime, if he had to, he'd kill Riley and his family in order to keep this time travel knowledge his secret.

Terry linked Riley's computer to his so Terry would be alerted anytime Riley accessed the "Time Hackers" program. Shortly after that, he gave Riley's computer back to Mr.

Clemmons so the organization could return it to Riley. Terry told his boss that the folder named "Time Travel" was Riley's attempt at designing a game.

Mr. Clemmons hadn't questioned Terry at all.

As Terry sat at his desk now, he felt a growing urge to eliminate Riley before the time-travel program got discovered by someone else. He knew he'd never get away with killing the kid at the present time. The police had too many ways of tracking down a killer. A hundred years earlier, before technology had given law enforcement DNA testing, blood-typing, and fingerprinting, it might have been possible. Besides, Terry wasn't sure he could really kill someone in cold blood. Instead, he mapped out a scheme to follow Riley through time and steal his computer. In effect, he would strand the kid in the past…260-million years in the past.

From information he'd gotten from Riley's files, Terry felt certain Riley had planned on visiting the Jurassic era. All Terry had to do was pop back in time at the same time Riley traveled, overpower the kid, and take his computer. Terry would then pop back home. No blood, no mess, and most importantly, no evidence. Sure, he knew Riley would be missed. The police would conduct a search, but Terry figured kids came up missing all the time. Riley would become another statistic, a cold case in the files of the law.

He glanced at his watch: 4:30. He needed to get Mr. Clemmons' report finished before going home. He had a strong feeling that Riley would travel back in time this weekend. It appeared he had already made a preliminary trip. And this next time, Terry was going to be ready to go with him.

JAKE Clemmons had stared at the door for a long time after Terry dropped off the report. *I can't believe he thinks he's fooling us.* He'd suspected Terry hadn't been telling him the truth from the beginning. The man couldn't lie worth a damn.

Not believing in putting all his faith in one place, Clemmons had employed his own personal computer expert and brother-in-law, Mark Peterson, to go through Riley's computer after Terry had returned it and before the computer was returned to the boy. Peterson had hacked into the folder named "Time Travel" in a month's time. Based on Riley's schematic, he built his own time machine. It had taken him a while to solve the problem of traveling to an exact location at an exact time, but now, he had perfected his machine to the point he could travel anywhere, anytime.

Clemmons had even taken a trip with him. They'd strolled the streets of Abilene in its heyday as a cow town in the Old West. He'd even gotten to see a gunfight. Two drunken cowboys faced off in the street at high noon. Fortunately, they were so drunk they couldn't hit the broad side of a barn, let alone one another. Their bullets went harmlessly into the ground or the sky. The sheriff had disarmed both of them and thrown them in jail. The following morning, Clemmons and Peterson ate breakfast with Sheriff Wild Bill Hickok. This once-in-a-lifetime moment for Clemmons bolstered his long-time infatuation with the Old West.

Clemmons had allowed Peterson free rein as far as where he went in time. He cared only that Peterson had the time machine working. Not that Clemmons had any specific plans with the machine, but he knew, if he wanted to, he could go back in time and do all sorts of crazy things and not get caught. He'd even fantasized about robbing a bank. It would be easy. All he'd have to do was appear in an exact location at a precise time. The location would be a bank vault in the middle of the night. There would be no need to break into the bank or the vault. Just pop in, grab the money, and pop out. In the morning, when the vault was opened and the money found missing, the police would have no leads.

Clemmons could even frame one of the tellers. He would go back in time and steal something personal from the unlucky teller, something that would leave no doubt about who had stolen the money. He would then plant it in the vault. No one would be the wiser.

Meanwhile, he'd bring the money back to the future and stash it away in a bank account in Sweden or the Caiman islands. The best thing about the plan, as far as he could tell, was that there was no way for him to get caught.

He shook himself out of the fantasy. He knew he could never stoop so low as to steal something that didn't belong to him, but he found it fun to think about. The time machine had other more important uses for now.

As the number-one man in his department, Clemmons didn't have to report to anyone except the President. He figured what the President didn't know wouldn't hurt him, at least for now. Once the information got out about the time machine, he'd never be allowed to use it. His gut feeling told him he needed to keep quiet about this for a little longer. He had a couple of other places he personally wanted to visit before he turned the information over to the President, who in turn would give it to the other departments of the government, who would more than likely squirrel it away for their own use.

Before anything else, however, he had one important task to perform with the time machine: keep an eye on Terry's time-machine activities. Because of the connection between Terry's and Riley's computers, he knew Terry was watching Riley's time travels. Although he didn't know why Terry was keeping track of Riley, he had a feeling Terry was up to no good. Without any evidence, Clemmons couldn't take action against Terry without a lot of government red-tape.

He was well aware that Terry had an obsession with finding a cure for his disease and would probably do anything to find that cure. *What better way than to travel into the future where science would be advanced enough to cure all of man's ills.* Terry's main problem would be keeping his time machine a secret, and that secret was already out.

Clemmons didn't think Terry was dumb enough to harm the kid or steal his computer in the present time, but if he were to track the kid's travel activities, he could be a danger to him in a different timeframe. Clemmons wasn't about to let that happen.

He pulled a phone number out of his wallet, a number penciled on a yellow Post-it note. There was no name, but he knew the person he was calling. "I have a job for you," he said when the phone picked up. "Meet me at the usual place at six-thirty."

The person on the other end of the line grunted and the line went dead.

CHAPTER 6

BACK in his room, Jeff closed the door and leaned against it. He sighed as he saw the animal lying on the blanket sound asleep.

"How'd it go?" Mitch asked without looking away from the game he was playing.

"Good, no thanks to you."

Mitch paused the game and turned his head. He glared at Jeff. "What's that supposed to mean?"

"She almost came up here when she heard this thing calling out or whatever it was doing. Couldn't you keep it quiet?"

Mitch huffed. "Not hardly. You try telling it to shut up next time and see how well it minds you." He resumed his game, dismissing the whole situation.

Jeff walked to the animal and stood over it. He knelt down and studied it in more detail than he had the last time. *Is this really a dinosaur? Could Riley and Wayne have gone back millions of years and brought it home with them?* He didn't know what to think. As he mulled things over in his mind, he chewed on his lower lip. He had to admit that it didn't look like any animal he'd ever seen or heard of.

When he stood up, the animal opened its eyes. A faint whine escaped from its mouth. Its brown eyes blinked and stared up at him.

The reaction reminded Jeff of the way a dog would whine when it wanted something. He felt sorry for the creature but didn't know what to do for it. He suspected it was missing its mom. A lump formed in his throat. Looking away, he blinked a couple of times to clear his eyes of the tears that had filled them. As much as he tried, he couldn't justify the presence of the ancient-looking animal. He couldn't come up with a logical explanation for it to be sitting in his bedroom and staring up at him. He hated to admit it, but maybe Mitch was right. Maybe it was a dinosaur.

Like cold butter on a hot skillet, Jeff's sorrow melted away to be replaced by fear as his mother called out, "Jeff, I need your laundry. I'll be back to pick it up after I've gotten Riley's and Wayne's."

He heard the door to his brothers' bedroom open. "Hi, boys." His mom's voice drifted down the hall. "It looks like you had a good day. This room is a mess."

"Dude," Mitch said as he nudged an elbow into Jeff's side. "Get your dirty clothes out in the hall before she gets back or you'll be in a world of hurt."

Shocked into action by Mitch's words, Jeff quickly gathered up his laundry. He put the hamper in the hall and closed the door. He stayed next to the door, just in case his mom decided to try to come in. He didn't know what he'd tell her, but he hoped to think of something while he waited for her to pass.

"Thanks, sweetheart," she called out a few minutes later.

Jeff sighed with relief as he heard her go down the stairs. Stepping away from the door, it swung open and hit his foot.

"That was way too close," Wayne blurted as he rushed toward the animal and knelt next to it, but not too close.

"Yeah, it was," Jeff stated angrily. Even though he was sure Riley didn't have a time machine, he knew he had to do something to get rid of the animal. He'd start by exposing the truth first. "Okay, Riley, go get your computer and let's see you take this thing back to wherever you got it."

"We can't go now," Riley said. "It'll be dark soon. I don't think it's a good idea to go at night. There's no lights. We can't see what's around us." He looked at Jeff with a serious expression. "Believe me, we *will* want to see what's around us."

"Yeah, dude," Mitch said obligingly, "let's go tomorrow when we'll be able to see everything." He smiled, nodding his head with approval at Riley.

Mitch's laid-back, easy-going California attitude irritated Jeff no end, but Jeff decided not to say anything about it at the moment. He turned back to Riley. "If you really have a time machine, just set the timer so we get there during the daytime."

"Well, I would," he said, bowing his head in embarrassment, "but I haven't quite figured out how to change my time of arrival that precise yet." Looking up again, he quickly added, "I'm working on it."

Jeff mimicked a chuckle. "So, you have a time machine, but you can't set it to arrive at a certain time." He mockingly winked at Mitch. "Sounds a little iffy to me."

"It has something to do with losing time as you travel through time," Riley explained. "The further back you go, the more time you lose. I'm working on the mathematics of it, but so far, I haven't been able to figure it out. I do know that if we go in the morning, it will be daylight when we get there."

Tomorrow was Saturday. His mom and dad were leaving him in charge for two days while they went to Vegas for a weekend getaway. *Two days. That should give me plenty of time to resolve this little problem.*

Wondering how they were going to keep the animal hidden from his parents all night, he said, "Fine, we'll go in the morning, but in the meantime, what are we going to do with that?" He nodded at the supposed dinosaur, which was now pushing the bedspread into a pile.

"It looks like he's settling in for the night," Mitch offered. "I think we should let him sleep where he is."

Dumbfounded, Jeff asked, "Are you nuts?" He turned to Riley. "We need to get him to your room."

"Not a good idea, dude," Mitch said.

"Yeah, she'll just walk into our room anytime," Riley said. "At least with you, she knocks before she comes in."

The more Jeff thought about it, the more he realized they were right. Besides, if he let the animal out of his sight, he'd lose control of the situation. As bad as he hated to admit it, he was stuck with the thing.

The animal finished piling up the bedspread and curled up

on top of it. Lifting its rear end slightly, it let out a loud fart.

"Great," Jeff said, rolling his eyes, "I get to sleep in the same room with a gassy dinosaur." He grabbed the can of air-freshener and sprayed it in a wide arc across the room.

Mitch smiled and crossed his heavily muscled arms over his chest. "So, what time do we leave tomorrow?"

Jeff knew they weren't really going anywhere to the past, just someplace to get rid of the dinosaur. For now, he figured the easiest way to put all of this behind him was to play along. "My parents are leaving for Vegas at eight-thirty. How about nine?"

"No can do," Mitch said, shaking his head. "Can't go until at least noon. I promised my dad I'd help him clean up the garage in the morning."

"Fine," Jeff said, aggravated that Mitch took all this so seriously. "And don't tell Macy. I don't want to deal with her and Carlita while we're trying to resolve this problem." Their two girlfriends were best friends, and Jeff knew if Macy found out about the dinosaur, she'd tell Carlita, then they would have a bigger complication on their hands. He couldn't help but notice that, as crazy as it seemed, he was starting to think of the animal as a dinosaur.

Mitch looked around at everyone. "I think we all need to bring a backpack with a few essentials, like a change of clothes, extra food, survival gear, stuff like that."

"Why?" Jeff said sarcastically, irritated that Mitch was taking the play-acting so far. "We're only going to take the dinosaur back, right?"

"Yeah," Riley said, "but it never hurts to be prepared." Quietly, he added, "Especially where we're going."

"That's right, dude," Mitch agreed, "just like the boy scouts: Be prepared." Holding his fist out, he tapped knuckles with Riley.

"Whatever," Jeff commented, his mind already working on how to keep the dinosaur hidden from his parents until morning. If he was lucky, his mom would be so busy getting ready for her upcoming trip to Vegas, she wouldn't have time to pay much attention to him or his brothers. They'd have to make sure the animal stayed quiet and he wasn't sure how to do that. Then, he got an idea. "Wayne, you and Riley see if you can sneak downstairs and get something to feed this thing." At their blank looks, he explained, "Anything…like lettuce, spinach, maybe broccoli. Keep trying until you find something it likes."

"What about some of the plants in the yard?" Wayne asked. "We could trim them. Mom and Dad wouldn't have to know why we were doing it."

"I don't know, dude." Mitch's eyebrows furrowed as he studied the creature. "I know some of those plants are poisonous, I'd hate to feed it something that might make it sick…or worse, kill it."

Wayne nodded in agreement.

Half Jeff's attention stayed on the conversation, while the other half wondered where his mom might be and what she was doing. Every now and then, she'd make a noise and he'd be able to pinpoint her location. At the moment, he heard the garbage disposal running in the kitchen. *Probably doing the dishes I was supposed to do earlier,* he thought guiltily.

"How are we supposed to get food if Mom's in the kitchen?" Riley asked.

"I'll distract her," Jeff said. He planned to catch her away from the kitchen and ask questions about things he should do while she was out of town. That would give the two boys time to do their thing. He counted on Mitch to keep the animal quiet until it got fed. "While you're at it," he said to Riley, "bring some water, too, This thing is going to be thirsty soon."

If they got through the night, Riley could come up with some excuse about something not working right with the computer. When that happened, Jeff and Mitch would take the animal out into the desert and turn it loose. *Heck, that's probably where it came from anyway. Now, to go talk to Mom.* "Everybody ready," he asked.

They all nodded as one.

"Okay, let's do this then."

CHAPTER 7

TERRY waited in the privacy of his office for an hour after the office closed to avoid the crowds that exited the building between 5:00 and 5:30. At 6:00, almost everyone was gone.

As Terry walked to his car in the parking lot, he thought about how his first three short trips through time had been so successful. He eagerly anticipated going into the future to find his cure, but first, he needed to do a little more experimentation and, more importantly, get rid of the kid. Once that was out of the way, he could start jumping forward in time to check out the medical advances.

On his drive home, he saw a couple of kids fighting in the street. It reminded him of a particularly bad day in junior high when he had been attacked by bullies. It had taken place nineteen years earlier when Terry was fourteen, a geek, and, unofficially, the most despised person in school. He hadn't cared what the other kids thought of him as long as they left him alone, which they did most of the time. That day, for some unknown reason, the school bully Chad White had decided it was pick-on-Terry day. Chad and his two friends, Rory and Pete, pestered Terry every chance they got. They would hide behind a door, jump out, and shout, "*Boo!*" Little did they know they didn't have to shout anything. Just their sudden appearance caused Terry to freeze.

Laughing, Chad and his friends would walk off, leaving Terry behind to pick up the books and papers he'd drop on the floor when his body froze.

Terry suddenly got an itch to travel back to that day to see if he could change things. As he passed his old high school, he stopped, grabbed a handheld GPS, and entered the building, still open with after-school activities and janitors cleaning floors. No one seemed to pay attention to him. He went to the bathroom on the second floor and recorded the GPS coordinates of the first stall.

After eating a quick dinner in his apartment, he sat at the computer with a baseball bat in his lap and punched in the GPS numbers, date, and time.

Instantly, he was transported into the bathroom stall just as Chad slammed fourteen-year-old Terry against the wall. Young Terry slid to the floor. Pulling his knees up, he placed his head on his knees and covered his head with his arms.

Older Terry stepped out of the stall. Without making eye contact with Chad or his friends, Terry swung the bat at Rory's head.

The bat connected with a dull thunk. Rory dropped to the floor with blood running from his scalp.

Pete spun around, but not fast enough.

Terry whipped the bat forward, catching Pete in the stomach. The force of the blow bent Pete over.

Terry hit him on the back of his head.

Pete joined Rory on the floor.

By that time, Chad had turned around and was crouched in a Karate stance in preparation for an attack.

Terry couldn't make eye contact or he'd freeze, nor could he hesitate and let Chad get the jump on him.

"Who are you?" Chad yelled.

Terry took two steps forward and swung the bat, breaking Chad's left wrist.

Chad moaned in pain. Holding his wrist with his other hand, he sank to his knees.

Terry swung again, hitting Chad in the face.

Chad's nose bent to the side and blood sprayed in an arc on the floor in front of him. Still on his knees, Chad shook his head from side to side, trying to clear his mind.

Terry took one more swing, this time aiming the bat at Chad's crotch. The tight corduroy pants outlined the target nicely. The bat connected with a sickening splat and Chad fell to his side.

"I'm the future, coming to get even," Terry said as he stepped back into the stall. Picking up his computer, he hit the enter button and arrived instantly back home.

Sweat poured from Terry's face as he caught his breath. He unsteadily sat down in his chair and set the computer on the desk. He'd never done anything violent like that before. His whole body shook...whether from fear or pleasure, he wasn't sure.

Thinking back on it now, he realized how risky it had been. He could have frozen. Chad, Rory, and Pete could have beaten the hell out of him. He could have been found by the principal and sent to the hospital. The cops could have gotten involved. How would he have explained why his driver's license and money were from the future?

Looking around, he wiped his forehead and sighed in relief. Despite the danger, he'd made it back safely. The thought brought a little smile to his lips. *I'm glad I did it.*

He remembered back to that actual day when he was fourteen. Chad had slammed him into the wall, but after he'd cowered down and covered his head, he recalled only vague sounds. Someone had come into the bathroom and beat the hell out of Chad and his friends. Young Terry had been too frightened to look up.

Now, Terry was glad he hadn't seen what had happened. It would have been too much of a shock to see himself standing with a bloody bat. In fact, both of them might have frozen up.

As Terry recalled, the principle never did figure out who had beaten up Chad and his friends. Now, it all made sense to Terry.

IT never ceased to amaze Jake Clemmons how many people ate at the food court in the mall. He found it a good place to meet because lots of people, noise, and distractions made it hard for someone to eavesdrop on a conversation. He took a sip of his coffee and winced at the bitter week-old taste. He added another sugar packet, hoping to make it drinkable.

"Coffee bad as usual?" a dark-skinned man said as he slid into the chair on the opposite side of the table.

"Worse. I don't think they've ever cleaned the pots. Either that or they see me coming and make a special pot just for me with an added splash of vinegar." He reached across the table and shook the hand of Eddy Tyrell. "How ya doin', E.T?"

"Can't complain." E.T. slouched down in his chair and stuck his long legs out, crossing his ankles. "And if I do complain, nobody listens anyway, so why bother?"

Despite his nickname, E.T. didn't look anything like an extraterrestrial from a distant place, unless someone considered Tucson, AZ, as distant. Beanpole thin and taller than most Hispanics, E.T. looked like he couldn't lift a six-pack of beer without help, but looks were deceiving when it came to this man. Clemmons had seen E.T. dead-lift a fallen comrade who weighed over two hundred pounds with all his gear. E.T. had not only picked up the guy and threw him over his shoulder, he carried him almost a half-mile to safety.

"What's up?" E.T. asked.

He never changes. Gets right to the point as usual. Clemmons leaned forward. Even though he felt secure talking here, he didn't want to be careless. "I recently acquired some technology that I think you're going to find quite intriguing."

E.T.'s bushy black eyebrows rose in anticipation. Sensing that something important was about to be said, he sat up straight and leaned forward also. His dark brown eyes became hard and serious. "Go on."

"Have you ever wanted to go back in time?"

E.T. ran a hand across his short-cropped black hair. "Sure, who hasn't? Why? You got a time machine?"

Clemmons glanced around. He lowered his voice even more. "Let's just say, hypothetically, I do. And let's say I am willing to let you use it. Where would you go and what would you do?" He watched his friend of twenty years closely. He felt he knew E.T. well enough to know what he'd say, but he had to be sure.

E.T. sat back in his chair. His eyes roamed across the room as his mind worked on the question. "I suppose, hypothetically, of course, that I would be tempted to use it for something evil, like robbing a bank or getting even with someone from my past." He took a drink of his coffee. "But in the end, I would use it to travel, see different cultures, like the Romans or the Aztecs in their golden days."

"What about going back to the Jurassic, seeing the dinosaurs up close and personal?"

"That would be interesting, too," he said hesitantly, as if he suspected what was coming.

"If you had access to technology like that, would you be able to keep it secret?"

E.T. scoffed. His mouth clenched in anger. "Hey, you know me better than that."

"Sorry, sorry," Clemmons said, putting up his hands to placate the man. "Just had to make sure, ya know."

As quickly as E.T.'s anger had come, it was replaced with curiosity. "So, do you have one?"

Clemmons leaned in close again. "Yeah, I do. And I need you to use it to protect a twelve-year-old boy and keep an eye on one of my employees. Make sure the employee doesn't do anything stupid and get himself killed."

"I'm all in. Tell me where and when."

Clemmons reached down and lifted the carrying case he had brought with him. He opened it slightly and gave E.T. a peek inside at the time-machine contraption: an alarm clock, GPS, and cell phone secured to the top of a laptop computer. "This is it. You'll need one or two other guys…guys you can trust with your life."

"No problem. I'll take Osborne and Taylor."

"That's who I was thinking you'd pick. Good choice. Now listen up, while I explain how to work this machine."

CHAPTER 8

JEFF'S dream girl slowly slid her arms around his neck. He closed his eyes in anticipation as her lips moved closer to his. Then, strangely, she licked the side of his face. Wondering why she would lick him, he opened his eyes.

He screamed and lunged backward, slamming into the wall.

"Wraaawoo, wraaawoo," the dinosaur screeched as it scurried across the room, taking refuge on its bedspread next to his desk.

"Oh, gross," he mumbled, wiping the animal's slobber off his face with the corner of his sheet. He swung his legs out of bed and glanced at the clock: 7:23. *So far so good. It's Saturday. Mom and Dad should be leaving pretty soon, then we can get rid of this stupid animal, one way or another.*

As if on cue, he heard footsteps in the hallway.

Someone knocked on his door. "Jeff, are you okay?" his mom asked, turning the door handle.

Fear-driven adrenaline coursed through his body as he rushed to the door. He reached it just as it cracked open. "Yeah, I'm fine," he said, peering at her around the edge of the door. "Why?"

"I thought I heard you yell," she said, scrutinizing him with her big baby-blue eyes.

"I…uh…I stubbed my toe…on my dresser."

The dinosaur bumped against his leg. Slowly pushing on the door, he hoped that if he shut it slowly enough, his mom wouldn't notice. With his right leg, he pushed the animal up against the door.

"Is your toe okay?"

"Yeah, its fine," he said trying to hold the dinosaur in place with his foot.

Walking away, she said, "You need to clean your room today. It stinks like an animal's been living in it. And what's with you kids and your loud T.V.'s lately?"

Sighing in relief, Jeff shut the door and looked down at the dinosaur. *If you only knew the half of it, Mom.*

IT was 10:30 a.m. in Washington, DC, as Terry piddled around the apartment and hoped he wasn't wasting his entire day waiting for Riley to fire up his "Time Hackers" program.

He had gotten up at six o'clock and had immediately turned on his computer, logging into Riley's laptop and waiting to be alerted when Riley accessed his program. Due to the three-hour time difference between Washington and Arizona, Terry figured he'd have plenty of time before Riley was awake.

Not wanting to miss the beep, Terry had even taken the computer into the bathroom with him. He hoped Riley wouldn't go back in time while Terry was sitting on the toilet. He mused that he wouldn't look all that menacing if, suddenly, he appeared in the past, crouched down with his pants around his ankles. Luckily, he'd finished his business, showered, shaved, and ate breakfast without being interrupted.

Now, over four hours later, he sat on the couch in his camouflaged pants, camouflaged long-sleeved shirt, and laced-up hiking boots with heavy lug soles. On the kitchen table sat his laptop time machine. On the floor by the table lay his backpack with a safari hat that he would wear when he was in the jungle. He'd spent over one thousand dollars buying top-of-the line camping gear, including a lightweight tent, sleeping bag, and dehydrated food. The salesman at the sporting-goods store had been helpful. After Terry's first freezing episode, the man had treated him with kid gloves.

Terry looked at the clock again. Time seemed to drag.

Maybe my intuition was wrong. Maybe Riley won't go back in time today.

Despite the delay with Riley, Terry realized he felt pretty good. In fact, it had been a long time since he had felt this good, mostly due to getting his revenge on Chad and Chad's toadies. He was prepared to take on Ryan.

He picked up the remote, turned on the T.V., and flipped through the channels to find something entertaining. He finally gave up. He moved his laptop to the desk next to his desktop computer and sat down to surf the internet on his desktop while he waited.

CHAPTER 9

AT 12:30 p.m. in Lake Havasu City, Jeff walked out of the house and into his parents' closed two-car garage. Wearing long pants, t-shirt, and hiking shoes, he looked around and silently cursed Mitch for being late.

Due to all the stuff the family had accumulated over the years, which took up one whole wall of the garage, Jeff's dad had to park his Dodge truck outside. In the open spot where the family car would normally have been parked, Wayne knelt on the floor feeding apples and bananas to the baby dinosaur. A thick rope had been attached to the animal's neck. *As if any of us could hold it if it wanted to take off.*

Wayne wore camouflaged pants with lots of pockets and a buttoned-down western shirt. Riley, dressed in Levi jeans, a long-sleeved shirt, and a Raiders hat, hunched over his computer at the workbench.

Jeff took a deep breath, trying to get rid of the irritation he felt at his brothers for getting him involved in this ridiculous mess. He wondered where they would be taking the dinosaur when this little game of theirs didn't work.

He walked to the workbench and threw his pack next to Riley's. Even though Jeff didn't believe they were about to go back in time, he'd packed a change of clothes, a Levi jacket, a small first-aid kit, a light lunch, and a canteen. He'd also thrown in a powerful Halogen flashlight and matches, just in case. If they didn't go to the past, he would be ready to go on the hike in the desert and let the animal loose. As he studied the creature again, he thought, *No, something tells me letting it loose is not a good idea. If this thing gets big, it might be dangerous to all living things.*

He leaned over and took a closer look at Riley's computer. It didn't look anything like a time machine. A digital alarm clock, a handheld GPS, and an old cell phone were duct-taped to the lid and connected to a coil of silver and copper wires that plugged into one of the USB ports. *What a piece of junk. The least he could have done is make it look decent.*

The side door opened and Mitch walked in, dressed in camouflaged clothing from head to toe. "Sorry, I'm late." He leaned a rifle case against the wall, then slid a huge backpack off his back and set it on the floor. "It took me and my dad longer to clean the garage than I thought."

Jeff couldn't imagine what Mitch had in his backpack. After his inspection of Riley's time machine, he knew, without a doubt, they weren't going anywhere anyway. He figured Mitch was just humoring the two kids.

At least, now we can get this over with. Riley will punch some buttons then make some lame excuse about something not working. Mitch and I can make Riley and Wayne take this...whatever...back to wherever they got it. Turning to Riley, he said, "Okay, hotshot, fire up your time machine and lets go."

"There's something I need to tell you before we go. We all need to–"

What's *that*?" a female voice blurted.

Spinning around, Jeff groaned.

Standing in the open door, which Mitch had neglected to close, was Macy Ann Grover, Mitch's redheaded, freckled-face girlfriend.

Jeff shook his head in disbelief. *Oh, crap, can this day get any worse?*

As Macy stepped into the garage, Carlita Juarez, Jeff's high-strung dark-haired girlfriend, followed.

Yep, it just got worse.

Dressed in sweats and running shoes, the girls had most likely been out for a run and stopped by to see what was going on.

Wanting to keep them as far from the strange animal as possible, Jeff hurried to meet the two at the door. "Carlita, Macy, what're you doing here? I thought you were busy all day today." He caught Mitch's eye and nodded at the open door, hoping Mitch would get the hint and help him get the girls back outside.

Mitch smiled and shook his head, his long blond hair covering his face with each exaggerated movement.

Taking the girls by their elbows, Jeff said, "You should finish your run. We've got things to take care of here."

Ignoring Jeff's words, Macy looked over her shoulder. "Is that a–"

"It's nothing. Don't worry about it." Jeff tried to guide them out the door, but they both pushed him away with disapproving looks.

Macy knelt down near the dinosaur. "It looks like a baby dinosaur, but…that's impossible, isn't it?" Her long red hair shimmered in the overhead florescent lights as she looked up at Carlita.

"Yes, it is." Carlita's brown eyes narrowed. She put her hands on her hips and looked suspiciously from Jeff to Mitch. "Which one of you is going to tell us what's going on?"

"We're busted," Mitch sang out. He grabbed for Macy as she stood up and tried giving her a kiss.

She impatiently pushed his bulk away. "I'm serious. What is this? Where did it come from?"

Knowing he couldn't keep it from them now, Jeff had them sit down and told them the story.

Macy looked like she believed it. Her emerald-green eyes glowed with excitement. "If you guys are going, we're going with you. Right, Carlita?"

Carlita had doubt written all over her face.

Mitch playfully winked at Carlita, then silently glanced at Riley and Wayne over his shoulder.

Getting the message, Carlita winked back and played along. "Sure, why not? It could be fun."

Not wanting the girls hanging around while they took care of the problem, Jeff said, "They can't go." Sarcasm dripped off his words. "They don't have survival packs."

Mitch pointed to his oversized pack. "I have enough for all of us."

Judging by the size of Mitch's pack, Jeff was sure he did.

Giving up on getting rid of the girls, Jeff said, "Fine, everybody come over to the work bench and let's get this thing over with."

As they gathered around Riley, he explained the rules. "Everybody has to have a direct connection to the computer when I hit the transport button. We all have to be touching, holding hands or something. Someone will have to link arms with me, since I'll be holding the computer."

Mitch raised his hand. "I have a question. Who's going to touch the dino?"

"I will," Wayne said as he stood next to the dinosaur and held the rope.

"I'm not sure I like the idea of you touching that thing," Carlita said. Carlita and Wayne had bonded from the first day they'd met. She considered him her little brother.

"It's okay, Carlita. I think he's starting to like me."

Carlita looked at Jeff with an unspoken message in her eyes: *If that thing hurts him, I'll hold you responsible and you'll be very, very sorry.*

Jeff took her hand. Pulling her next to him, he leaned over and whispered into her ear. "Don't worry, Wayne knows what he's doing. He'll be careful."

She patted his cheek and tipped her head slightly to the side. "For your sake, you'd better hope so."

Jeff knew he was in pretty deep. He just hoped he could smooth the whole thing over without any lasting repercussions.

The guys gathered their packs. Everyone got in place with Jeff and Carlita to Riley's right, and Mitch, Macy, Wayne, and the dinosaur to his left.

Making sure they were touching each other, Wayne held the rope and reached a hand down, resting it on the dinosaur's head. "Ready whenever you are, bro," he called out.

We must look ridiculous, Jeff thought as he held Carlita's hand and linked arms with Riley. *I'd like to have a picture of us standing here like idiots. I could torment Riley for years.*

Then Riley hit the button.

Jeff screamed as a painful blast of brilliant yellow light hit his eyes.

FIVE minutes earlier, Terry sat hunched over his desktop computer when his laptop beeped and lit up. The sudden noise startled him. He froze for only a second as he realized what the beep meant. Riley had accessed the "Time Hacker" program.

Terry's pulse raced. *It's about time.*

He grabbed the laptop and set it in his lap with shaky hands. He had to be in direct contact with the computer in order to be transported back in time. He couldn't be sure that he would be transported along with Riley, but if not, he would have to punch in his own coordinates and time, which he could copy from Riley's entries.

Terry suddenly realized he'd left his backpack sitting next to the kitchen table. He hated to think of what would happen if he went back in time without his pack full of brand new survival gear.

Picking up his laptop, he hurried to the kitchen and set it down on the table. He picked up his backpack and put it on one of the chairs while he looked around to make sure everything was in order.

Damn, I left the desktop computer on. He knew it wouldn't hurt anything to leave it on, since he'd be coming back at almost this exact moment in time, but he couldn't stand the thought of leaving without turning it off.

He quickly checked the laptop. Riley had accessed the program, but he hadn't entered a time period.

Terry rushed back to his desk. He was shutting down the computer when his laptop beeped three times, the signal that Riley was one click away from jumping through time.

Terry quickly hit the power button on the desktop and shot back to the kitchen. Just as he picked up the laptop, he saw a flash of blinding light. One last brief thought passed through his mind. *Oh, no, I wasn't touching my backpack.*

CHAPTER 10

THE yellow light, brighter than the sun, burned into Jeff's eyes. Red hot spikes burrowed into his brain. Groaning in pain, he jerked his hands free of his companions and grabbed his head. Bending over, tears ran down his face. He sank to his knees and massaged his temples. He heard Mitch and Carlita moaning. *As soon as I can see, I'm gonna kill Riley for this.* He felt a small hand on his shoulder.

"Sorry, Jeff," Riley said, "I forgot to tell you to close your eyes."

"Why should that matter?" Mitch asked in agony nearby.

"I don't know," Riley replied. "It's some quirk about time travel. Maybe we aren't meant to see how it happens. But don't worry, it doesn't last very long."

"Great," Jeff said sarcastically. As the pain faded, he sensed something different around him. The air felt heavy with humidity. Buzzing insects and grunts of animal life hit his ears. He inhaled a musty, earthy smell, mixed with the sweet scent of flowers.

Suddenly, the pain disappeared. He opened his eyes. He blinked rapidly to clear the tears. *Wait a minute. We should be in the garage. How come I'm kneeling on grass?*

Slowly standing up, he stared in awe at the sight before him. They stood on the edge of a clearing about a hundred yards across. It was filled with lush grass and surrounded by giant flowers and thick, tall jungle-like vegetation. A babbling brook ran through the center of the clearing and disappeared into the plant life to his left. The land looked fairly flat. At least he didn't see any hills from where they stood. Downstream, a mountain loomed in the distance.

Feeling disoriented, Jeff took it all in and tried to come to terms with it. *This can't be real. This can't be due to Riley's time machine...but then again, I don't have a logical explanation for it either.*

"Wraaawoo, wraaawoo," the baby dinosaur called out. As soon as Wayne untied it, it dashed off, crossing the stream and diving into the bushes.

"That's gratitude for you," Riley said flatly. "He didn't even say goodbye."

Mitch laughed. "He probably wanted to get out of here before you zapped him somewhere else."

Wayne piped up, "I wonder if the light hurt his eyes, too?"

"There's no way to know, bro." Mitch wiped at his eyes as if what he was seeing was a trick that would disappear with enough wiping. Blinking repeatedly, he shook his head. "I didn't really believe it, but Riley's time machine works. This is awesome."

Beaming in pride, Riley said, "Of course, it works."

"Oh, it's so beautiful," Macy said, looking all around her, her green eyes filled with wonder.

Noticing Macy's eyes not watering, Jeff said, "Didn't the light bother your eyes?"

"No," she answered, "I thought the trip might be windy, so I closed them."

Jeff couldn't help but laugh. He liked Macy, but sometimes she said the stupidest things. Even though she had red hair, he liked to kid her that sometimes she acted like a stereotypical dumb blond.

"What's so funny?" Macy asked, frowning with hurt at his laughing.

"Nothing," Carlita said sharply, her face drawn and pale, her eyes wide in fear. She stood stiffly. Her voice quivered. "This isn't real. It can't be. Riley, whatever you did, undo it and take us back to your garage."

"But it is real," Riley insisted.

"It looks real to me," Macy commented. "Come on, let's look around. I want to see a big dinosaur."

Carlita stomped her foot. "No. We need to go back. Right now."

Mitch set down his backpack and gun case. He put an arm around Carlita's shoulders and led her toward the center of the clearing. He had a gift for being able to calm down anyone, anytime, anywhere. Jeff couldn't hear what Mitch whispered, but he knew whatever it was, Carlita's shoulders relaxed.

Still confused that they had traveled through time, Jeff felt an unquiet anxiety of his own, but he didn't want to be the one to complain. He stepped close to a colorful plant and studied it. Nine or ten feet tall, it sprouted broad, spiked leaves. Eight-inch purple flowers with yellow centers grew from the base of each leaf. Knowing nothing about plants, he couldn't tell if it was prehistoric or not. He did recognize the ferns, palms, and evergreens. The trees in the distance looked like redwoods. Under a bush with long, straight shafts and perfectly rounded leaves, a group of yellow mushrooms grew.

"I don't think I'd try eating those if I were you," Mitch said nonchalantly as he approached Jeff.

Irritated Mitch could be so easygoing about this whole thing, Jeff silently turned and watched Carlita and Macy tentatively wander around the clearing. Carlita still seemed a little nervous. He said to Mitch, "Doesn't it bother you at all that we're not in my garage anymore? Aren't you the least bit curious as to what just happened? I mean, look at this." He swung his arm in an arc. "Where the hell are we?"

Mitch brushed back his blond hair. "Hey, it is what it is, bro. Who am I to question what happened? I'm willing to accept the fact that we traveled back in time to the Jurassic era. Why can't you?"

"It's just too unbelievable," Jeff muttered. "It's not possible, is it?"

"Dude, whatever the mind can conceive and believe, it can achieve. If we think it's possible, it is. So, let's go explore, see what's out there."

A deep rumbling roar came from the bushes to their left.

Spinning, Jeff's heart raced in fright. Whatever made the noise remained hidden by the thick brush. It sounded big…too big. He gulped as it dawned on him that, if this world was real, it could be just as dangerous as it was beautiful.

"Relax, bro," Mitch said as he opened his gun case and pulled out a lever-action rifle. He popped the protective covers off the scope and jacked a shell into the chamber with practiced ease. Patting the stock of the rifle, he said, "This is a 375 H & H magnum, the one my dad used to kill that Cape Buffalo two years ago in Africa."

Jeff mentally compared the size of a water buffalo to a full-grown T-Rex, and didn't believe for a moment that Mitch's rifle would protect them from a large dinosaur. "Even a small dinosaur's a lot bigger and tougher than a buffalo, isn't it?"

CHAPTER 11

TERRY hadn't gotten his eyes closed soon enough. The bright light still burned a hole in his head. He'd experienced the light the first time he'd gone through time, so he knew it would disappear quickly. Holding his computer with one hand, he rubbed his eyes with the other. As the pain decreased, he blinked the tears away and looked around. Surrounded by a mixture of brush, ferns, and pine trees, he stood on what looked like a long path about five feet across.

Where's the kid?

He heard someone groaning in pain, then faint voices came through the thick brush. Apparently he'd arrived at the same time as Riley, but he didn't understand why he'd been transported to a different location. Something had gone wrong on his computer. He'd have to recalculate his figures when he got back home. He only hoped that it was Riley he was hearing and not someone else.

Working his way toward the voices, he moved slowly and quietly, but the brittle fallen leaves and twigs underfoot sounded to him like a herd of elephants tromping through a layer of dry branches. In the areas cleared of debris, he picked up his pace as he headed toward the voices.

He wished he'd brought his backpack full of supplies that he'd spent so much money to purchase, but once he grabbed the kid's computer, he could pop back home and wouldn't need it.

He heard a deep rumbling roar from somewhere to his right. He paused, one foot lifted in the air. Whatever it was, it sounded huge. *I better make this quick. I don't want to run into any animals that live here.*

He cautiously made his way toward the voices, now only a

few feet away behind a wall of brush. Crouched down, he held his computer in one hand while parting a bush with the other.

He silently gasped at the sight of six kids. He'd expected Riley to bring maybe one or two of his little friends. As he watched, he knew the kid with the glasses and computer was Riley. He'd seen a picture of him on the kid's computer. The smaller boy and one of the older boys were probably Riley's brothers. They had similar features. The presence of the two teenage girls in sweats and running shoes surprised him.

The two older boys looked to be in their mid to late teens. The one with the long blond hair and bulging muscles appeared particularly huge and menacing. He even held a rifle.

Terry hadn't counted on guns. He felt his muscles tightening up. If he weren't careful, he'd have a freezing spell. He needed to keep himself calm.

He heard another roar, this time closer—close enough to make him freeze for a few seconds.

I need to hurry and get this done, he told himself, *but how can I with all these people?*

He listened carefully. They seemed to be arguing.

"We did what we came for, so let's get going," the older brother said.

The youngest kid whined, "Can't we stay and look around for a little while?"

The redhead seemed to agree. "Jeff, I don't think it would hurt anything to stay for a little while."

Taking two long angry strides, Jeff yanked the computer out of Riley's hands. "This place is too dangerous. We're going home, even if I have to figure this thing out and take us back myself." He opened the computer.

"It's password protected," Riley said with a smirk. "There's no way you can turn it on."

Punching the keys, Jeff swore in frustration when nothing happened. He glared at the blond hulk who had come with him, then sent the computer flying back to Riley, who caught it in midair.

Darn, Terry thought, *I wish it would have fallen and*

broken. That would have saved me a lot of trouble.

Terry got the impression most of the group wanted to stay and look around. He felt torn. If they stayed, he would have a better chance that Riley would wander off and Terry could snatch his computer. On the other hand, Terry didn't like being in this strange, unpredictable environment. The thought of dinosaurs scared him. He wanted badly to go home.

"I know, you've got a gun," Jeff yelled at the other male teen. "Big deal. So did that guy in *Jurassic Park* and look what happened to him. He died." He stomped away from the group in irritation, coming straight toward Terry's position.

Terry could feel his muscles trembling, on the verge of freezing. It took all of his concentration to prevent it.

Luckily, the kid stopped and turned his back to Terry.

Terry forced his breathing to stay light. The last thing he needed was to be discovered before he was ready to act.

"I'll tell you what," Riley said, "let's look around for one hour, then we'll go home. I promise, we won't go very far and we'll be very careful."

All but Jeff and the dark-haired girl slowly moved next to Riley as though silently making their votes.

"Four to two," the big guy said. "Looks like you've been outvoted, bro."

When the last girl hesitantly joined the group, Jeff threw his hands in the air. "Fine, but if one of us gets killed, I'm not going to take the blame for it."

Terry could see well enough through the bush to know each of the boys had a backpack. The long-haired teen had an extra-large one. For their sake, Terry hoped they had everything they needed to survive because they were going to be here for a long, long time.

E.T. opened his eyes and quickly surveyed his surroundings. He'd taken two previous trips back in time to get used to the process so he could concentrate on this mission. Clemmons and Peterson had hurriedly programmed the computer to deposit the three mercenaries roughly a quarter-mile west from where the kid's computer had identified his location. The other target, Terry, would be just east of the kid.

Osborne took the left flank. His short, compact body looked smaller than normal under all the gear he was wearing.

Taylor's large figure took the right flank.

Just like we rehearsed, E.T. thought as he one-handedly swept his M-16 in an arc from right to left and looked around for threats.

"Clear," Osborne's voice said in E.T.'s earpiece, followed closely by Taylor's, "Ditto."

"Roger," he said into his mike.

Taylor returned and put the computer in E.T.'s backpack. All three of them had their own time-machine computer, just in case. None of them wanted to be stranded 260-million years in the past because of a stupid mistake.

E.T. checked his compass. "Move out." He strode quickly, silently through the vegetation toward the estimated location of the targets. He'd been in Iraq, Afghanistan, and numerous other places with alien countryside, but he'd never encountered grunts and growls like those assaulting his ears now. They created disturbing pictures in his mind.

Suddenly, a three-foot-tall dinosaur came rushing out of the brush just ahead of them. As they stood in shock, it detoured around them on a dead run.

"That's a baby Triceratops," E.T. said in amazement.

"Little guy's in a big hurry," Taylor commented.

"Hope nothing big is chasing it," Osborne replied, his deep, bass voice unusually calm under the circumstances.

"Let's stay focused, guys," E.T. said. "We've got a mission to complete."

"Just saying," Taylor added, "I don't want to run into a T-Rex lookin' for an easy meal."

With his big meaty hand, Osborne patted the grenade launcher attached to his rifle. "We do, I'll feed him one of these."

"Enough chatter," E.T. barked impatiently. "Whatever we

come up against, we'll handle on a case-by-case basis." He looked at Osborne. "Remember, we're to remain incognito. No shots unless absolutely necessary."

"Yes, Sir," both men blurted while coming to attention and throwing mock salutes.

E.T. cracked a smile. He'd been in some tough situations with these two and, even though they could be a little unruly at times, he knew he couldn't trust anyone more than he trusted them.

Turning his attention back to their mission, he caught a glimpse of sunlight flashing off an object in the clearing ahead. He held up his hand and sank to a crouch. With his binoculars, he slowly panned the area. *There it is again.* He saw movement...people.

Moving stealthily ahead, he stopped at the edge of the clearing where he easily spied the kid's group about seventy-five yards away. Among them were two teenage males, two teenage females, and two little kids. From the pictures gathered on the family, E.T. recognized Riley, Jeff, and Wayne. He figured the others were friends of Jeff. *Good grief, six kids is more than we bargained for.*

"One gun visible," Taylor whispered.

E.T. hoped the teen with the gun didn't hear them and get trigger-happy, shooting at E.T. and his men. *I'd hate to have to shoot him.*

CHAPTER 12

ANGRY at the cluster of his companions standing against him, Jeff still felt jittery about staying. When he thought he heard movement in the nearby bushes, he turned to look.

Macy screamed behind him, "Ahhhhh, get it away from me."

Spinning around, Jeff saw Carlita frantically swatting at a bumble bee the size of a sparrow buzzing around Macy's head. At the same time, something roared again behind him, sounding closer. Jeff's heart pounded as he nervously stepped away from the bushes.

Mitch rushed to help Carlita and Wayne shoo the bee away. Mitch kept an eye on the bushes, too, for whatever animal might be lurking there.

"I think it was attracted to your hairspray," Wayne said to Macy as they watched the bee move to a patch of red and orange flowers.

The deep rumbling roar sounded again. This time, it was growing closer, either moving toward them quickly or made up of a large number of animals.

The hair on the back of Jeff's neck stood up. "We did what we came to do," he said crossly as he scanned the bushes, expecting a dinosaur to come charging out at any moment and attack them. "The baby dinosaur's home. It's our turn to go home. Riley, get your computer ready. Let's get out of here."

As he headed toward the group, he heard something moving in the bushes behind him, something *big*.

Macy looked over his head and screamed.

Jeff froze, not turning around. He pictured a T-Rex poised above his head, six-inch teeth ready to tear him to pieces. He tried to move, but couldn't. Never in his modern, civilized, safe life, had he been so terrified.

WHEN the girl screamed, something hit Terry from the side and knocked him over. In shock, he dropped his computer in order to use his hands to break his fall. Worried about the time-machine computer being broken, he grabbed for it just as a foot, the size of an elephant's, crashed down and covered half of it.

He stared in disbelief at the computer, bent and smoking. The cell phone had been crushed and the clock had been knocked off. A chill ran down his spine. He knew, without a doubt, his computer would never work again and he didn't have the means to repair it.

The huge foot lifted off the computer as the dinosaur took another step forward and stopped.

Terry tilted his head back and looked up at the creature's monstrous underbelly, which stood high enough from the ground that Terry could almost stand up straight without hitting his head. Not wanting to get stepped on and smashed like his computer, he slowly crawled away from the underbelly and stayed near the ground twenty feet away.

Numbly staring at his useless computer, Terry couldn't believe the tables had been turned. Instead of stranding Riley in the past, Terry would be stranded. He didn't even have his carefully selected survival supplies to help him.

Now, Terry had only two options. One, he could show himself to Riley's group, confess as to why he had followed them, and hope they would take pity on him and let him travel back with them. Two, he could follow Riley, separate him from the pack, steal his computer, then go home.

Definitely the second option.

PARALYZING fear locked Jeff's joints, keeping him from running. Everything around him seemed to move in slow motion.

Riley waved his arms and screamed, trying to scare the dinosaur away.

Mitch raised his rifle to his shoulder.

Jeff's mind screamed, *Yes, Mitch, please shoot it. Kill it before it eats me.*

Riley, Carlita, and Macy watched in terror, their faces contorted, certain Jeff was about to die.

Jeff wondered, *Does time always slow down just before you die?*

Wayne stepped forward and shoved the muzzle of the rifle into the air, causing Mitch's bullet to sail harmlessly away.

No, Wayne, why did you do that?

A sudden shove from behind Jeff roughly propelled him forward. After falling, he scrambled to his feet and ran. Time and movement returned to normal. Arriving safely with his companions, he spun around to see the dinosaur that almost ate him.

About twenty feet tall, a long curved horn projected from the nose upward between the eyes and above the head by about a foot. Its skin, gray with a dark strip on the top of the neck and back, looked tough and leathery. With a low, long groan, the dinosaur turned and walked away.

THE deafening gunshot startled Terry so thoroughly, his body froze up for a good fifteen seconds. With the shot so loud and so close, he thought the group might have seen him and were shooting at him.

The huge animal picked that moment to leave. It turned and walked away while Terry remained unable to move. Its tail swung to the side, knocking Terry head over heels. He rolled along the ground before the side of his head slammed into a rock.

Terry knew he had to get up. He had to follow Riley, if for no other reason than to let Riley know he was here and needed help. He didn't want Riley to leave him behind. He didn't want to be the only human on earth.

He fought the darkness, but it was useless. He let out a silent scream as he drifted off into unconsciousness.

CHAPTER 13

NOW out of danger, Jeff turned to Wayne heatedly. "Why did you shove Mitch's gun?" he yelled, his voice shaking from the near-death experience. "Why didn't you let him shoot it?"

"It was only a harmless Parasaurolophus." Wayne shrugged his shoulders. "I knew it wouldn't hurt you."

"A pair a what?" Macy asked in confusion.

"A Parasaurolophus, a Hadrosaurid," Wayne explained casually, as if this tidbit of dinosaur info was common knowledge. "They eat plants, not people."

Carlita said to Wayne, "I recognized it from the books I used to read to you when you were younger."

It all started to come together in Jeff's mind: Wayne's fascination with dinosaurs since he was four, Riley's time machine, and a baby Triceratops in his brothers' bedroom. "You convinced Riley to bring you back here, to this exact period in time on purpose, so you could see real dinosaurs up close and personal didn't you, you little twerp?"

"So what if I did?" Wayne shot back. "Wouldn't you have done the same thing if you had the chance?"

"No, I wouldn't. I wouldn't put my life or anybody else's life in danger just to look at some stupid dinosaur."

Mitch interrupted the argument. "Come on, it's over now. Let's go look around."

Jeff put his hands on his hips. "I can't believe you're going to stay here after what just happened. What if that would have been a T-Rex?"

No one spoke, but no one turned to Riley to get him to go home, either. Even high-strung Carlita seemed to indicate she wanted to stay.

Jeff sensed he was stuck. Disappointed, he said, "Okay, we'll stay, but just for an hour, and only if we can go somewhere that's more open, I don't like being in this small clearing, surrounded by tall bushes and trees. We can't see what's around us."

Wayne, seemingly thrilled that the close encounter with the Parasaurolophus didn't change anyone's mind about staying, ran to the nearest tall tree. "I'll take a look from up here. I should be able to see if there's a big clearing close by."

"Be careful," Carlita called out as Wayne started up the tree.

"There's only one problem with leaving this area," Riley stated, catching Jeff's immediate attention. "We have to come back to this exact spot to go back home. Otherwise, we won't end up back in our garage."

"So, who cares where we end up?" Macy asked. "As long as we get home, what does it matter?"

"It matters a lot," Riley said somberly. "What if we suddenly appear in Wal-Mart? Don't you think people might be a little upset?"

"I doubt it," she replied. "I see some pretty strange people in that store sometimes."

"But I doubt if any of them carry big backpacks and a rifle." He pointed to Mitch.

"The dude's right," Mitch said. "It wouldn't be good to just pop up somewhere."

"Hey," Wayne yelled from the upper branches of the tree. "I can see a huge open area over that way." He pointed in the direction the brook flowed.

"How big is it?" Jeff hollered.

"*Big*. It reminds me of what Africa must look like. Wide open plains with lots of animals grazing. There's also a big lake." He made his way down the tree.

Carlita asked. "How far do you think it is?"

"I don't know…a mile…maybe two." Reaching the ground, he joined the excited group.

"Two miles?" Jeff muttered, shaking his head. "I can't

believe you want to go two miles from here." He wondered where they would end up if they walked the two miles, then had Riley zap them back home. *We'll probably end up in some old couple's living room, scare the shit out of them, maybe give 'em both heart attacks. Well, at least we'd be home and safe.*

"What're we waiting for?" Mitch said enthusiastically. "Let's go see some dinos. I'll take the lead, since I have the gun. Riley and Wayne follow me. Jeff, you bring up the rear behind the two girls, okay?"

"How are we going to make sure we can find this place again?" Riley asked, seeming particularly concerned that they get back to this spot.

"Easy, dude," Mitch said as he pulled a machete out of his backpack. "Jeff'll make marks on the trees we pass. All we have to do is follow the marks back."

"Kind of like Hansel and Gretel," Carlita said. "Only instead of bread crumbs that can be eaten, we're leaving marks that are guaranteed to be there to show us our way."

"That's right," Mitch said, handing the machete to Jeff.

Jeff hefted it, feeling its weight. "So, what do I do? Make a little cut on the bark or what?"

"No, not a little cut," Mitch said, taking the machete back. "A *big* cut. We want to be able to see it from far away." He stepped to the nearest tree and swung the blade on a slightly downward angle. He wiggled the weapon back and forth to remove it from the bark. Swinging it again, coming upward this time, he took a four-inch-by-six-inch V-shaped notch out of the bark. The light wood interior of the tree stood out boldly against the dark brown outer bark. "Think you can handle it, dude?" He handed the machete back to Jeff.

"Yeah, I don't think I'll have any problems," Jeff replied.

"Oh, one more thing," Mitch added. "I'm leaving my rifle case here, right where we came in so we know where to go out. I'm going to be really pissed if we can't find our way back to get it, so make sure you put the mark on the tree *after* you pass it. That way we'll be able to see it easy on our way back."

"No, duh," Jeff shot back. "You just lead the way and

don't worry about me." Jeff secretly hoped Mitch *did* worry about him. In fact, he hoped Mitch was worried about all of them. He didn't want to admit it, but he was still scared from his recent experience with the dinosaur.

"Wait!" Riley yelled. He sat down on a fallen tree and opened his computer.

"What are you doing now?" Jeff asked, hoping Riley had changed his mind and was going to take them home.

"I'm going to change my password."

"Do you have to do that now?" Mitch asked.

"Yes, I do. I have to cut and paste my current password from one of my pictures. I want to change it to something I can type in fast if I need to."

"Makes sense to me," Carlita said.

It wasn't long before Riley stood up.

"You done?" Mitch asked, antsy to go.

"Yup."

Mitch walked to the front of the group and started down the trail with the others following him.

Bringing up the rear, the machete in Jeff's hand made him feel a little braver. Still, it wouldn't do any good against a large predator like a T-Rex. Heck, it wouldn't do much good against anything bigger than a small dog. If there were such small dinosaurs, he didn't know if they would attack a human or not.

Roughly following the brook southward, Mitch led them away from the clearing.

Face it, dude, Jeff thought as he started off behind Macy and Carlita, *you don't know anything about this place.*

When Mitch had marked the tree, it had looked easy, but it took Jeff six swings to mark his first tree. He ran to catch up with the group or risk being left behind.

E.T. watched as the group of kids lined up and started off down the creek. The last boy, Jeff, carried the machete.

"Looks like they're going exploring," Taylor said with a

sigh.

"I know. I feel the same way," E.T. replied, wishing the kids would have decided to just return home for their own good, not only with Terry on the loose, but also after the dinosaur scare. They had been prepared to shoot the big creature standing over the kids, but the animal hadn't been menacing. He still felt uneasy about the whole ordeal. "I have a feeling things are about to get really interesting. Come on, let's go. We don't want to let them get too far ahead of us. Who knows what's waiting for them around the bend." He stood up. "But, hey, look on the bright side. If things go horribly wrong, we'll be the first men to kill a dinosaur with a rifle."

"I'd rather not," Taylor replied. "I really doubt if our rifles will stop a large, angry, charging dino, and I'm wearing too much gear to outrun one. I'd rather just confront these idiots and make them go back home where it's safe."

"We need to break up so we can cover everybody," E.T. said. "Osborne, you stay on Terry, who is now Target Two. We'll cover this group."

"Roger, boss," Osborne said as he immediately took off on a course that would take him to the north of the clearing and keep him out of sight of the kids.

A growl from something very large somewhere in the area sent chills down E.T.'s spine. He had a bad feeling about this mission, but he'd never quit a job yet. Adjusting his pack, he made his way across the clearing and cautiously followed the kids' trail.

CHAPTER 14

GROANING, Terry reached up with his eyes closed and gently explored the area on his head that felt like someone had stuck a knife in it. Wincing in pain at the touch, he decided not to probe the wound further. He felt the wetness of blood on his fingers.

A strange sniffing, huffing noise by his feet caught his attention. It sounded like a dog sniffing.

Cracking open one eye, he lifted his head.

A blurred group of animals scurried away from all around him.

Scared he was surrounded by a pack of wild dogs, he quickly sat up. The landscape swam before him as his head tried to keep up with his body. He kept both hands on the ground to keep his balance.

As his vision stabilized, he sucked in a breath of fear. A group of strange animals had formed a circle around him and quietly watched him. About two feet tall, their bodies appeared similar to a modern-day dog, but their heads resembled a lizard. Instead of fur, scales like a snake's covered their skin. He counted some twenty of them. He preferred a pack of wild dogs, animals that were at least familiar to him.

One of the larger animals started making a high-pitched, cackling, laughing noise that sounded like a hyena. One by one, the pack members joined in, all of them laughing so loud it hurt Terry's already pounding head. He wondered if the animals were getting ready to attack or just voicing their displeasure he was still alive. *If I stand up, they might find me more menacing and go away.*

He rolled onto his knees and prepared to stand. His eyes didn't focus right as bolts of pain shot through his head. He closed his eyes and shook his head to throw the pain off like an old blanket. When he opened his eyes again, he could see more clearly, which he took as a good sign. An even better sign was the big stick lying on the ground in front of him.

The animals had stopped making noises and watched him closely.

Terry took a firm grip on the stick and used it to push himself to his feet. Swaying a little, he turned in a slow circle.

The largest animal, the leader, took one step forward.

Terry knew enough about animals that if he showed any fear, he'd be attacked en masse. Gripping the stick in both hands like a baseball bat, he lunged forward and swung at the leader of the pack. It reminded him of hitting Chad and his toadies.

His swing perfectly hit the animal on the side of the head. It dropped to the ground without making another sound.

Seeing their leader fall, the other animals resumed their strange laughing noises. This time, it was accompanied by a shrill whistling noise that Terry guessed to be a warning call. The animals converged on their leader, surrounding him.

To Terry, it appeared some of the animals were poking and prodding the fallen one, trying to get him to stand up. Others formed a circle, facing outward to protect the leader.

Terry didn't know much about dinosaurs, but their loyalty surprised him. He'd figured they would abandon an injured member and run off to save themselves. Whatever the case, this was his chance to get away and get back to the business of Riley's computer. He backed up to the wall of brush. With none of the animals paying attention to him, he turned and pushed his way through the brush to the clearing.

He stopped and stared in disbelief. Riley and his friends were gone. *No, it can't be,* his mind screamed. *How long was I unconscious?*

It wouldn't have taken Riley long to reprogram his computer and go home. The big dinosaur might have frightened them away.

A great dread passed over Terry that he was stranded

forever with no survival gear. He stood paralyzed for several seconds.

When he started to gather himself, he walked to the area where the kids had been standing. He noticed the gun case. He picked it up. "Why would they leave this?" he said to himself. "Did they forget about it?"

He looked around. He saw a fresh cut on a tree. It looked like a hatchet cut. *Maybe they stayed after all. Maybe they went to look around.* He began to feel a sense of relief, but he didn't want to get his hopes up too high.

Dropping the gun case, he studied the ground, thick with grass, leaves, and small twigs. The grass had been crushed where the kids had stood. He looked for signs of which way they might have gone, moving toward the tree with the freshly cut bark. *Jackpot.* Leading away from the tree and into the brush along the creek, he found unmistakable fresh signs of the kids, moving in what looked like a single file.

At the small stream, he saw a clear footprint in the mud, the footprint of a tennis shoe or running shoe. His hope began to rise. They were still here. He could feel it in his bones.

Heck, tracking isn't so hard, he told himself as he bent to get a drink of the sweet, cool water. *I can do this. I'll find Riley. I'll steal his computer. I'll go home.*

Filled with a sense of pride and new courage, he set out on the trail Riley and his group had foolishly left for him.

"TARGET Two is moving south," Osborne said into his mike as he moved out of his hiding place and started stalking Terry, who walked south along the bank of the creek.

Earlier, Osborne had wondered if they had failed on the part of their mission to keep Terry alive. Terry hadn't moved for ten minutes and Osborne had been about to check on him when Terry rolled over and groaned. It was a good thing, too, because that group of nasty dinos looked about to eat him whether he was dead or not.

Don't think E.T. would've liked that. He peered from

behind a tree and watched until Terry was out of sight before he moved again. *Nope, E.T. would never forgive me if I'd watched while the dinos killed the man I was supposed to be protecting. Hell, I'd never forgive myself.*

Though Osborne had been only thirty feet from Terry, he'd blended into the scenery with his head-to-toe jungle camo, including his gear. Sitting in the middle of a large green bush with lots of purple and green flowers, not much of him was left visible. He was glad he'd waited, because Terry managed to get himself out of the mess.

How Terry had swung that stick, killing one of the dinos, impressed Osborne. *The guy's got guts. He may not be as helpless as we thought. We don't want to underestimate him if we have to confront him, nor underestimate his danger to the kids.*

Osborne came to an area where those ahead of him had been forced to go to the edge of the water because of a thicket of brush with two-inch thorns spaced every few inches along the branches. In the mud next to the water, he clearly made out the footprints of the kids. The lug soles of army-issue hiking boots worn by E.T. and Taylor were different enough from Terry's hiking boots that Osborne had no problem telling their tracks apart. He wondered if Terry had even noticed there were two extra sets of footprints in the mud.

He doubted it. As far as Terry knew, only six other people had come into the world at this point in time. Why worry about who left what tracks?

Osborne got a drink from the creek. He knew from firsthand experience how important it was to stay hydrated in this kind of heat and humidity.

CHAPTER 15

JEFF kept looking back at each mark he'd made. When he thought he was far enough from the last mark, he'd make another one. Looking back had another benefit: watching for dinosaurs that might sneak up behind him. He looked back a lot. He wasn't sure why they needed to mark the trail since they were traveling next to the brook, but he figured Mitch knew what he was doing.

As the day wore on, the temperature and humidity rose. Before long, all of them sweated heavily.

After traveling what seemed to Jeff like five miles, they stopped where the brook slowed and widened. The vegetation thinned. Clumps of ferns, and bushes were spaced about ten to twenty feet apart. *Enough space for a person to run unimpeded, should a dinosaur come along.* Scattered randomly through the brush were trees of every size, from seedlings to monsters hundreds of feet tall and probably twenty or thirty feet around. The biggest ones looked like redwoods. Some of the smaller ones were normal pine trees, but next to the redwoods, they seemed puny.

"Let's take a break for a few minutes," Mitch said. "I want Wayne to climb another tree and see how far it is to this open area we've been looking for."

"I'm on it, boss," Wayne said, scampering toward the biggest pine tree in the area.

"Yeah," Macy said, plopping her butt down on a moss-covered log. "I swear we've walked at least a couple of miles."

Jeff sat next to her. "Why are you complaining? Don't you and Carlita run like four miles every day. This should be nothing for the two of you."

"Yeah, but it's not this humid at home," Macy responded, wiping the sweat off her forehead with the sleeve of her sweatshirt.

"It's no wonder your overheating," Riley remarked. "You ought to take your sweatshirt off."

"I can't," she said, blood rushing to her lightly freckled face. "I don't have anything on under it but my sports bra, and I'm sure not going to run around in front of you boys wearing just my bra."

"I'm thinking seriously about doing just that," Carlita said, wiping her face as well. "I don't know how much longer I can take this heat." Her long black hair hung in wet tendrils from her forehead.

"While we're waiting," Riley said, "why don't you at least go over to the brook and splash some water on your head and get cooled off."

"Good idea," Carlita said. "We can get a drink while we're there."

Macy wrinkled her face up in disgust. "We can't drink that water. It's not clean."

Mitch laughed. "Macy, that water's probably cleaner than any water you've ever had."

"Well, I'm still not going to drink any," she said with finality as she got up.

As the two girls walked to the brook to cool off, Wayne came back from his scouting trip. "It isn't much farther," he said, stopping next to Mitch. "Just over the next few little hills."

"Cool, dude. Thanks a lot." Mitch hi-fived his little bud.

"I'm gonna get a drink," Wayne said, heading for the brook. "Then we'll get going again,"

"Why should we keep going?" Jeff asked Mitch. "Why don't we finish up the hour here, then go home." Looking at his watch, he tensed with surprise to see how much time had passed. "We've already been in this world over an hour."

"Relax, dude. We still have plenty of time before it gets dark, so we might as well take our time and look around while we can."

"But you said one hour."

No one paid attention to him or seemed to care about prolonging their stay.

Frustrated, Jeff followed the girls and knelt down next to Carlita, who stared into a calm section of the brook. "So how's the water?" he asked.

"Rippled," she said, pointing at the water's surface.

He looked down. The water was rippled, all right, and as he watched, the ripples grew bigger. *Hmm, I wonder what could make the water ripple like that?*

The ground under his feet began to vibrate.

He and his companions instinctively moved closer to each other, each one's face revealing the same fear he felt that something terrible was about to happen.

E.T. sensed something wasn't right. He slowly scanned the jungle, his eyes flitting over the vegetation and looking for anything out of place.

Next to him, Taylor did the same. "You feel it, too?"

"Yeah."

"What is it?"

"Don't know for sure," E.T. said as he moved close to a large tree. "But I think we need to stay here for a minute until we figure out why we're feeling this way." He put his back against the tree.

Taylor went on watch on the other side.

With a full 360-degree view between them, E.T. tried to figure out why he felt so uneasy. He concentrated on the sounds coming from the jungle. Off to his left and right, things sounded normal, but in the direction they'd just come from, all was quiet…too quiet. *Maybe it's because Terry and Osborne are still behind us,* he thought as his eyes scanned the vegetation again. *But it wasn't quiet when we came through, so why would it be quiet now?* He had a sneaky suspicion it involved the animals, which seemed to know something was about to happen.

"I'm thinking we need to go up the tree," Taylor whispered.

"Go, I'll cover you."

Taylor handed his rifle to E.T. and jumped as high as he could, barely able to reach the lowest branch.

E.T. heard a grunt as Taylor lifted himself and his gear onto the branch.

"Okay," Taylor said, his voice betraying the effort it took to get him and his gear ten feet off the ground in ten seconds.

E.T. passed Taylor both rifles and jumped for the same branch. Almost effortlessly, he pulled himself up and scurried past Taylor until he was a good thirty feet off the ground, gathering his rifle as he passed by. "You're getting soft, Taylor," he said without the slightest hint of strain from the eight-second assent. "Or old," he added with a chuckle, knowing it would hit a nerve.

"Old, my ass," Taylor shot back. "I'll outrun, out-climb, and out-fight you any day of the week you–"

"That's enough, soldier." E.T. hadn't thought Taylor would be so touchy about his age or he wouldn't have kidded him. He'd have to watch what he said from now on. *Or maybe he's just on edge and nervous like I am.* It wasn't natural to travel back in time millions of years. He couldn't blame any of them for being a little edgy.

Remembering that some dinosaurs stood well over thirty feet tall, he climbed a little higher. From his new perch at seventy feet in the air, he could see clearly down into the brush. He spied Terry, picking his way along the creek on the path E.T. had just come over. Osborne patiently followed behind him. What did surprise E.T., though, was the cloud of dust rising into the air just behind Osborne.

CHAPTER 16

"WHAT'S going on?" Jeff called out to Mitch, the one with all the outdoor skills and hunting experience.

Normally cheerful, Mitch looked around with concern. "I'm not sure, but whatever it is, I don't like it."

A rumbling noise came from the north. As it grew louder, animals grunted, squealed, and honked.

Terrified, Macy slid next to Carlita and held her arm. "I'm scared," she said trembling.

Riley and Wayne stood apprehensively, looking to Mitch and Jeff to decide what to do.

"Quick, everybody," Mitch said, "follow me that way." With his rifle, he pointed westward into the brush.

Suddenly, a large Parasaurolophus came charging out of the brush, headed downstream. It nearly knocked Mitch over.

The rumbling grew louder and the earth seemed to shake.

"I think I know what's going on," Mitch said over the noise. "It's a stampede. We need to get out of here, like right now." He shoved Carlita to get her moving, then grabbed Macy by the arm and took off running toward the west.

Stunned, Jeff hesitated.

A ways away, another dinosaur charged through the brush. It knocked down small trees without even slowing down.

The noise from moving animals grew so loud, Jeff barely heard Riley yell, "Come on, Jeff, *move it!*"

A shove from Wayne finally got Jeff moving. He started out in the direction of Mitch, but a group of four dinosaurs forced him and his brothers to run the other way. With four large dinosaurs threatening to stomp them into the ground, Jeff ran, blindly following Riley and Wayne, ducking and weaving through the bushes. They splashed through the brook then headed due east.

Dividing his attention between following his brothers and evading the dinosaurs coming up behind him, Jeff looked for a large tree they could climb, but unfortunately, he saw nothing climbable within view. The pine trees in this area were all too small and the redwoods didn't have branches low enough to reach.

He glanced over his shoulder again. One of the dinosaurs was getting close. "Go left," he screamed to Riley in the lead.

Riley dodged left.

The dinosaur roared past them like a runaway locomotive.

Jeff felt his legs growing weak and shaky. More dinosaurs passed, maybe hundreds or thousands in the herd.

He wondered how much longer he could keep up this pace.

FIVE minutes earlier, Terry heard a rumbling in the distance but didn't pay much attention to it. His head throbbed. He wished for some Excedrin or Tylenol to dull the pain. He swatted at the pesky buzzing flies, no doubt attracted to the fresh blood still seeping from his head wound. If he had only grabbed his safari hat with the net attached before he'd left home, he could have kept the flies away from his face and neck.

All around him, the animal noises seemed to rise, adding to the pounding in his head. He stumbled forward along the brook, still following the footprints and signs of the kids.

The place was a wonder with its untouched vegetation, huge flowers, and gigantic ferns. *I could make trillions of dollars bringing scientists back in time to study the wide diversity of plants and animals, not only in this time period, but every time period since time began. I could charge higher prices for the further back in time someone wanted to go. A dollar for every year. You want to go back 150-million years? No problem. That'll be 150-million dollars, please.*

He felt giddy just thinking about it as he swatted at the flies.

The loud rumbling noise coming up behind him drew him out of his reverie. He paused and listened. He began to hear the sounds of individual animals. As the rumble grew louder, his heart pounded faster.

A dinosaur suddenly burst through a wall of brush and ran past him in a hurry.

What the hell's going on?

Two more dinosaurs ran by, both looking like they were running for their lives.

Then it hit him: they *were* running for their lives. Whatever was chasing them was headed in his direction. Turning at a ninety-degree angle, he jumped the creek and plowed into the brush, running at least a half-mile before the stampede passed.

Thinking he was clear of the mad rush, Terry slowed down to a walk.

Suddenly, he heard more dinosaurs come crashing through the thick brush. When two big creatures appeared just twenty-five feet in front of him, he panicked and froze.

The two animals split off to the sides of him as they approached, leaving him open to a smaller one, relatively the size of an African elephant, which didn't so much as flinch when its front leg slammed into Terry.

Like a football having been punted by a football player, Terry sailed gracefully through the air. He collided with a huge redwood tree. He heard his left arm and a rib break on impact. The soft layer of pine needles carpeting the ground caught his fall. *Why does this always happen to me?* he wondered as he passed out…again.

MITCH half-dragged Macy by the arm and ran as fast as the two girls could go without falling. Looking back for Jeff, Riley, and Wayne, he almost got himself and the girls trampled. *All I can do is hope they don't get hurt. We'll worry*

about finding each other later. He swerved around a bush and jumped a fallen log, almost losing his rifle. Luckily, they didn't have to run too far. Most of the dinos went in the opposite direction. After a half-mile or so, Mitch stopped.

Panting from the exertion of running with a fully loaded pack on his back and his rifle in his hands, Mitch took a moment to catch his breath and said, "Whoa, dudes, that was intense. I never thought I would have to run from a herd of stampeding dinos."

Both girls, bent over gasping for air, gave him dirty looks for calling them *dudes*.

He knew they hated it, but he loved to called them *dudes* just to piss them off.

Carlita reached up with both hands and pushed the sweat-soaked hair off her terror-stricken face. She said in a shaky voice, "That wasn't intense…that was scary."

Mitch shrugged. "Whatever. I thought it was cool."

Macy said nothing.

Suddenly worried she might have been hurt while they were running, Mitch looked at her.

White-faced, her green eyes were wide with fright. Her body visibly shook.

Mitch put his arms around her and held her tight. "You okay, babe?" he whispered in her ear.

She nodded, her face rubbing against his chest. "We were wrong to stay. We should have listened to Jeff and gone home. Can we go home right now, please?"

He patted her back. "I wish we could, sweetheart, but we need Riley and his computer to do that."

Stepping away from him, Macy stood straighter. "Come on then. Let's go find the others." She wiped her eyes and sniffed.

Mitch could tell she was putting on a brave front so he wouldn't worry about her.

Resting the rifle in the crook of his elbow, Mitch turned and started back the way they had come. He silently agreed with Macy…maybe this hadn't been such a good idea.

E.T. felt like a god watching the events of the stampede as they unfolded in the jungle underneath him. From his perch in the tree, he could see not only Riley and his group, he'd caught glimpses of Osborne, too. He'd lost track of Terry.

Osborne had gotten separated from Terry and called E.T. on the radio for instructions.

"Stay where you are for now. Once everything settles down, we'll go find them again."

One branch below him, Taylor said, "Uh, oh, boss." He pointed toward the north, where the stampede had come from.

E.T. saw why the dinosaurs had been running. His mouth clenched tight as an uncharacteristic wave of fear washed over him. He hoped the kids would keep running. He wanted them nowhere near the ferocious T-Rex stalking along the back trail of the stampede and looking for something to eat. *Knowing* there were dinosaurs like the T-Rex out there and actually *seeing* one, were two different things. He half-feared to get out of the tree, but he had a job to do.

"We need to split up. Taylor. Go find the group that went to the east. I think Riley and his brothers went that way. I'll go west, after the other male teen and two girls. Remember, don't interfere unless it's a matter of life or death."

"Gotcha, chief." Taylor quickly made his way down the tree and took off in a ground-eating lope.

"Oh, and Taylor?" E.T. said on the radio.

"Yeah, boss?"

"Watch your back. There may be more than one of those T-Rexes out there."

"Oh, great."

When Taylor didn't say anything more, E.T. figured he was either too busy running or too busy watching for dinosaurs. Before he climbed down the tree, E.T. called Osborne and told him what was going on. "Keep following Terry. Just don't let him see you." E.T. didn't have to remind either man that they weren't supposed to be seen, but for some reason, he felt if he didn't, one of them would react too soon and blow their cover.

"Roger," Osborne's deep voice rumbled in his ear piece.

Leaving the creek, E.T. broke into a gentle run, hoping he could catch up to his group of kids before they ran into something big, mean, and hungry.

CHAPTER 17

WHEN the dinosaur herd slowed and stopped, Jeff dropped to his knees in exhaustion. As he finally caught his breath, he said, "Are you guys okay?" He looked at Riley and Wayne for obvious injuries.

"Yeah…" Riley panted, his computer tucked under his arm, "I…I think so."

"I'm glad you didn't lose your computer," Jeff said.

"Me, too," Wayne blurted, his face pale with fright. "This place is dangerous. I want to go home"

"Well, I'm glad somebody finally agrees with me." After a brief rest, Jeff stood up. "Okay, lets head back and see if we can find Mitch and the girls."

Pushing himself off the ground, Riley said, "I hope you remember the way back, because I don't. Do you, Wayne?"

"Are you kidding? I was too busy running to pay attention to where we were going."

"We'll just follow our tracks," Jeff said, walking in the direction from which they had come.

It didn't take him long to figure out that following their tracks wouldn't work. The stampeding dinosaurs had erased all traces of human footprints from the ground. Jeff decided to follow the dinosaur footprints instead. Unfortunately, the animals had run in every direction. Their tracks crisscrossed so much, it was like they'd run back and forth in their panic. The vegetation was sparser here than it had been where they'd started running.

"Why don't we take a bearing on the sun or something?" Wayne suggested after they'd been walking around for a few minutes.

"What good will that do?" Jeff said. "Even if we know which way north is, there isn't anything to use as landmarks to get us back where we started. Besides, I don't know if we ran east or south. For all I know we ran in a big circle and are only a hundred yards from where we started."

Dejectedly, and obviously exhausted, Wayne fell silent.

Riley said, "I think we should walk for fifteen minutes in each direction and mark trees as we go with the machete. If it doesn't look like we're heading in the right direction, we'll come back and try another way."

Jeff felt the burden of responsibility weighing him down. "I guess that's all we can do for now." After marking a tree, he led his brothers in the first direction.

As he walked, it dawned on Jeff just how much he'd relied on other people to make decisions. There had always been someone he could turn to for advice or help. Being alone with the responsibility for the lives of his two brothers scared him. One wrong decision, one wrong move, and they could all die instantly. His pulse raced. His eyes began to blur as a panic attack began to set in. Concentrating on his breathing, he told himself, *It's going to be okay. It's going to be okay. We have the computer. We just have to find Carlita, Mitch, and Macy. Then, Riley can zap us home.* He didn't care if they ended up in Wal-Mart or somebody's living room, at least they'd be back in their own time period where nothing could eat them.

After walking for fifteen minutes, they came to a section of brush growing so tightly together, they couldn't have come through it.

Riley stopped and adjusted his glasses. "This can't be the way we came."

Jeff looked at his watch. *This isn't good. It's almost 3:00. Judging from the position of the sun, it probably gets dark here around five or six. That only gives us an hour or two to find Mitch and the girls.*

Wearily, Jeff turned around with his brothers. As he began walking back to their starting point, he wondered how Mitch and the girls were doing. *Poor Carlita, she must be scared out of her wits. She'll probably be so angry, she'll break up with me when we get home.*

MITCH was amazed at the amount of damage the stampeding dinos had done to the vegetation. It looked like a giant hand had reached down from the sky and swept across the land, flattening everything but the tallest trees. The sweet smell of crushed bushes, plants, and flowers contrasted sharply with the rancid smell of huge stinky piles of dino dung that had been deposited along the escape route. There were so many piles, in fact, Mitch figured they could fertilize half of Kansas. He wondered if the dinos dropped them on purpose, trying to lighten their load to run faster or to distract whatever had been chasing them.

Macy and Carlita stayed close to him, one on each side.

Passing near one of the piles, Macy pinched her nose and said, "Oh, that is so gross."

Holding her nose, too, Carlita said, "I thought a baby's poop was stinky, but this stuff is really bad."

"Hey, look there," Mitch said, stopping the girls.

A group of small bird-like dinosaurs ran through the trampled brush, stopped at one of the piles of dino dung, and started eating it.

"Oh, gross," Macy mumbled. "I think I'm going to be sick." Heaving, she held her hands across her stomach and turned her head away.

Laughing, Mitch said, "Hey, that's just part of nature. Waste not, want not."

Slapping him on the arm, Carlita said, "Come on, let's get moving before Macy loses it. I don't want to watch her throw up."

Mitch was surprised when a new group of dinos came running from behind them. Far enough away that Mitch didn't need to take shelter, they stampeded in the opposite direction this time. *Maybe they got confused and turned around while they were running.* He shifted his rifle to the crook of his other arm.

Macy clutched his arm tightly. After watching the dinos

go by, she turned to Mitch, her voice serious. "You know Jeff was right. This place is too dangerous. When we find them, we need to go home."

"I agree, totally," Carlita added. "I want to go home where it's safe."

Mitch watched a dragonfly, the size of a seagull, cruise past. "I want to go home, too, but until we find Jeff and the boys, we're stuck here. We just have to use our heads and treat the land and animals with respect."

"*Respect*?" hollered Macy. She stomped her feet in anger. "How do you show respect to a dinosaur that's trying to eat you? You can't. All you can do is run like hell and hope he doesn't catch you. This world," she said, moving her arm in a wide arc, "is as alien to us as Jupiter or Saturn. When it comes right down to it, we don't know squat." Her face turned red and her green eyes glittered with tears.

Mitch realized she was scared of dying in a foreign land where she wasn't supposed to be. Ashamed for not paying more attention to her feelings, he put an arm around her shoulders and pulled her to his chest. Resting his chin on her soft red hair, he whispered, "I'm sorry, babe."

Sniffling against his chest, she murmured, "That's okay. I'm sorry I yelled at you. I'm just scared and want to go home."

Underneath his macho, southern-Cal, laidback exterior, Mitch knew he was really a big, sensitive teddy bear, but he kept it hidden. Only a few people knew. Macy was one of the chosen few who knew his secret. "Tell you what," he said guiding her to a fallen log, "let's take a break for a few minutes. Then we'll go find Jeff and go home."

CHAPTER 18

AS Jeff, Riley, and Wayne retraced their steps back to the hub where they had started, Jeff worried that they weren't going to find Mitch and the girls before it got dark. Luckily, he'd had some survival training lessons at summer camps, but he'd never really put much stock in the training nor thought he'd ever have any use for those skills. He mentally went over the few things he'd thrown into his pack before they had left home: a change of clothes, a small first-aid kit, a light lunch, a flashlight, and matches. At the time, he hadn't really thought Riley's time machine would work. Now, he wished he'd brought a big pack like Mitch's with a tent and bedrolls.

The thought of spending a night with huge, carnivorous dinosaurs prowling around in the dark made him cringe. He didn't know which would be worse: losing one of his brothers to a dinosaur or having to tell his parents about it. The overwhelming burden of responsibility continued to weigh heavily on his shoulders. A flash of white-hot anger shot through him at Riley for pulling him into this mess. He also felt angry at Mitch for getting separated from them.

Jeff glanced at Riley, his body fatigued and his eyes full of fright. Jeff knew it wouldn't do any good to yell at him. All Jeff could do now was keep them alive until they found Mitch and the girls. Then, hopefully, they could all go home.

By the time they finally reached the spot where they had started from earlier, Jeff's anger had evaporated, unlike the sweat soaking his clothes and dripping from his forehead. Emitting a sigh of relief, he dropped to the ground on the shady side of a bush. His stomach rumbled. He had emptied the water in his canteen a while back so he had nothing to quench his thirst.

Riley and Wayne looked just as tired, hungry, and thirsty.

Leaning his head back, Jeff said, "Why don't we take a five-minute break before starting out in another direction?"

Mumbles of approval from Riley and Wayne convinced him to stay at least five minutes, if not longer. He closed his eyes and concentrated on relaxing his muscles, but the ominous silence of the primal forest kept his nerves on edge.

A strange rising and falling grunt drifted across the lush green landscape.

Jeff tried to imagine what the creature looked like, but something told him he'd rather not know.

MITCH sat on the log next to Macy and, trying to soothe Macy's concerns, talked about things back home.

Macy wiped the tears from her eyes, but they only seemed to get worse.

Carlita scooted next to her and put an arm around her shoulders.

Mitch had hoped that talking about something familiar would calm Macy down, but it didn't seem to be working. Racking his brain to think of something else to lighten her mood, he glanced around for something non-threatening.

A huge butterfly, the size of a dinner plate, flitted through the air in their direction. Its patterned wings of red, blue, and green flashed in the sunlight.

"Look." he pointed. "Not everything here is dangerous."

Macy looked up briefly, then started sobbing again.

Carlita gave him a thanks-for-trying-anyway smile.

Mitch got up and, resting his rifle in the crook of his left arm, picked a dozen huge flowers from a nearby bush. Eight inches in diameter, each flower displayed a bright yellow center with light-pink petals, trimmed in a band of dark purple around the edges.

As he returned to the log, Macy and Carlita stood.

Mitch handed the bouquet to Macy.

The huge flowers filled her arms. Despite the tears dripping down her cheeks, her eyes lit up. She gave him a warm smile as she silently mouthed, "Thank you."

He felt his face turning red and bowed his head shyly.

Suddenly, Carlita grabbed his arm. "Mitch," she muttered in fear as she yanked on his shirt sleeve.

Whipping his head up and around, Mitch's eyes widened in surprise. His mouth dropped open.

Eighty feet away, stood a T-Rex. It didn't look happy.

JEFF could feel his leg muscles cramping. If he didn't get up and get moving, he'd stiffen up. It made him realize he wasn't in as good of shape as he'd always thought. When he and Mitch worked out, Mitch would tell him, "Come on, dude, no pain, no gain." *Well, I ought to get a lot of gain out of today,* he told himself as he forced himself to his feet.

Seeing a tall pine tree, maybe a quarter-mile away, he asked his brothers, "What do you think? Should one of us climb that tree and see where we're at. Maybe we can spot the others."

Wayne, lying on his back in the middle of a crushed shrub, shaded his eyes as he opened them. He mumbled, "Whatever you decide is fine by me."

A little more lively, Riley got up with his computer. "That sounds better than running around here, hoping we can figure out where we are. From up there, maybe we can see the lake."

Jeff held his hand out to Wayne. "Come on, let's go." He pulled the reluctant Wayne to his feet.

"I'm thirsty," Wayne whined.

Jeff turned and started off toward the tree. "Me, too. Let's see if we can find a Seven-Eleven and get us a Slurpee somewhere along the way."

MITCH, swallowing down his panic at the sight of the T-Rex, softly said, "Don't move and be quiet."

The girls stood behind him.

The T-Rex's sides heaved from an apparently long run. It swung its massive head back and forth. Stretching out its neck, it sniffed the air as though looking for prey.

This must be why those dinosaurs were on the run, Mitch thought as he slowly reached his hand toward his rifle, still cradled in the crook of his arm.

The dino's head stopped moving, pointing right at Mitch and the girls.

"Uh, oh," Carlita whispered, her body shivering. "I think it smells us."

Bellowing, the creature charged toward them, covering ground surprisingly fast.

Not having time to raise his rifle and fire off a shot, Mitch turned to tell the girls to run.

They were already twenty feet away and moving fast.

Doing the hundred-yard dash in what he thought was world-record time, Mitch risked a glance over his shoulder.

Even though the T-Rex appeared to be exhausted, almost limping, it still gained on them.

Putting on a burst of speed, Mitch closed the gap between himself and the girls. "Faster," he screamed as he came up behind them. "It's catching up."

A roar, too close for comfort, motivated Carlita and Macy to find new reserves of speed.

Jumping brush, logs, and rocks, the trio ran for their lives.

Close behind, air rushed in and out of the T-Rex's open mouth. Its footsteps pounded the ground.

Mitch expected to feel its teeth sink into his back at any time. His lungs burned. He forced himself not to look back, not wanting to take the chance. If he tripped, he'd be history.

Gradually, the sounds of the T-Rex started to fade.

Mitch began to think that they were going to get away. *The dino must be too exhausted to keep going*, he thought, feeling like he'd been running for hours himself.

Just as everything seemed to be opening the way for their escape, Macy tripped and fell.

CHAPTER 19

ON the trek to the tree, Jeff heard the gurgles of a small spring bubbling up between two rocks. Realizing his extreme thirst, he rushed to the spring and dropped to his knees. Scooping the water up with his hands, he drank the sweet, cold water, relishing the taste as it quenched his thirst.

Wayne lay down on his stomach and put his face right into the water as he noisily slurped it up.

Riley stood above them. "I wouldn't drink too much all at once," he warned. "You'll end up sick."

Wayne didn't stop long enough to acknowledge him.

Jeff didn't care. He would drink until he was full.

Riley knelt down and drank a few handfuls.

When Jeff finished, he sat back against a fallen log. "*Ahhhh*, that was good." He wiped the excess water off his face.

Wayne got up and sat on a large rock. Patting his stomach, he said, "Yeah. Not as good as a cherry Slurpee, but it's good enough."

Shaking his head, Riley scooped up a couple more handfuls of water.

Suddenly, Jeff's stomach lurched. He put his hand on it, wondering what was happening. Abruptly turning to the side, water sprayed from his mouth over the grass. Wiping his mouth, he looked up just in time to watch Wayne give a repeat performance.

Riley chuckled. He raised his hands to his mouth and took another small a sip of water. "I told you not to drink so much so fast. Your stomach can't handle that much water all at once. Not only that, it's bad on your kidneys."

"You could have told us why," Jeff retorted in anger.

"I know you two," Riley stated philosophically. "It wouldn't have made a difference."

"All I know is, I'm thirsty again," Wayne said, kneeling down to get another drink. This time he slowly sipped out of his hands instead of gulping.

After Jeff took a small drink and filled his canteen, he said, "Let's get to that tree and see where we are. Hopefully, we can figure out where Mitch and the girls are, too."

MITCH stopped to help Macy. He grabbed her arm, lifting her to her feet. Quickly glancing over his shoulder, he saw the T-Rex was only fifty feet away.

The animal took deep ragged breaths, then slowly walked toward them.

"*Go, go, go,*" Mitch urged, pushing Macy.

She took a step and crumpled to the ground with a grunt. "I can't," she said in a panic. "I twisted my ankle. I can't walk on it." She looked up at him, tears of fear and frustration running down her face.

Mitch waved to Carlita to keep going.

The brief rest must have revitalized the T-Rex because it let out another roar and charged again, but at a slower pace this time.

"*Stand up, now,*" Mitch yelled as he reached out and grabbed Macy's hand. Yanking her to her feet, he picked her up in a fireman's carry. The pack on his back and the rifle on his arm made it awkward, but there was nothing he could do. Groaning as he lifted the extra hundred pounds, he staggered off quickly with the T-Rex in pursuit.

For Mitch, it had turned into a test of endurance: Mitch versus the T-Rex. He vaguely remembered that the T-Rex was supposed to be a sprinter and would give up a chase fairly quickly. *So, why is this thing still chasing us?* he asked himself as he nearly tripped on a branch. *Because it still thinks it has a chance to catch us? That means I've got to figure out some way to lose it.* The extra weight slowed him down, allowing the T-Rex to gain on them.

Macy's voice quavered with fear as she hollered, "Mitch, hurry. He's getting closer."

"I'm going as fast as I can," he wheezed between breaths. He didn't know how much longer he could keep up this grueling pace. Sweat ran into his eyes and blurred his vision as he looked ahead, hoping to see something he could use to help them lose the T-Rex, like a growth of trees too thick for the animal to break down, a pile of boulders they could climb, a tight underground tunnel they could crawl into. Hell, right now, he'd welcome anything that would get them to safety.

Even with the extra weight of Macy on his back, he was catching up to Carlita, now some thirty feet ahead of him.

Suddenly, Carlita tripped and fell.

No! his mind screamed. *There is no way I can carry her, too.*

Carlita quickly jumped to her feet, hardly losing any ground.

Mitch sighed in relief as he dodged the brush and bushes in front of him. This put him at a disadvantage to the T-Rex, which just mowed through the bushes like they weren't even there.

"M-M-Mitch," Macy stammered. "*Ahhhhh.*"

Her ear-shattering scream came just before he heard the T-Rex's teeth gnash together right behind him.

Shockingly, Carlita was now running toward them with her eyes wild and her arms in the air.

Fearing she was going to sacrifice herself so they could get away, Mitch yelled, "No, go back. What are you doing?"

Ignoring him, she ran toward the T-Rex and threw a softball-sized rock at it, hitting it in the left eye.

Roaring in anger and pain, the creature turned its attention to her.

Mitch stopped for a moment, getting a better grip on Macy.

As Carlita led the T-Rex in another direction, Mitch realized she had picked up the rock when she fell. Then it dawned on him: She hadn't fallen at all. She had picked up the rock on purpose. "What a girl," he muttered under his breath.

Mitch readjusted Macy on his back and set off walking in the direction Carlita had gone. He only hoped she could stay ahead of the T-Rex until it got tired and gave up the chase. He worried to think what would happen to her if it caught her.

CHAPTER 20

TERRY slowly came back to consciousness. Before he opened his eyes, he lay completely still and listened to the sounds of the forest. *Where am I?* Squawks, howls, and grunts seemed to come from a myriad of animals in every direction. He remembered hitting the tree and hearing bones crack.

Reeling with pain, he slowly rolled to his right side, using his right arm to push himself into a sitting position. Holding his left arm tightly to his aching side, he managed to get to his feet.

He carefully pulled the sleeve of his shirt up to his elbow and inspected his left forearm. No bones stuck out of his skin. He probed with his fingers to determine whether or not the bone was displaced. As far as he could tell, it was a clean break. If he were careful and didn't injure it further, it would heal on its own.

Turning his focus to his side, he felt pretty sure only one rib had broken. He winced at the pain caused by his poking. *At least, it doesn't feel that bad*, he thought. *These injuries won't kill me.*

He turned his attention to his surroundings. Ears attuned for the slightest human sounds, he turned in a 360-degree circle, hoping to see some kind of sign telling him where Riley and his group had gone.

A memory flashed through his mind that he'd run from Riley's group when the dinosaurs had stampeded. He thought now that it might have been wiser to get behind a big tree and let the dinosaurs go past like rush-hour traffic on a freeway. That way, he wouldn't have lost track of where he had been.

As usual, Terry had panicked instead of using his head.

He had to get back to the creek to figure out the direction Riley might have taken. But first, he had to decide which way to go in order to find the creek.

He moved to where he'd been when the dinosaurs had come crashing through the brush. Orienting himself, he started walking. He soon found one of his footprints in a bare patch of dirt. Confident he was heading in the right direction he shuffled along.

At this point, he had grown really tired of this world and wanted to go home. He didn't care who was with Riley when he found the boy. Terry decided he would grab the computer and start punching buttons until he traveled back home or was shot and killed. With the computer in his hands, he was pretty sure they wouldn't shoot him...at least not until they realized he was going home without them. Then, no doubt, they would try to kill him.

Maybe I should just grab the computer and run. When I'm alone, I can program it to take me back home.

THE vegetation grew thicker, but luckily, Mitch could easily follow the trail the T-Rex had made through the brush.

Not far ahead of him, he saw the backside of the T-Rex.

The creature roared.

Mitch took a short detour on another path until he was halfway past the dinosaur and peered through the leaves.

Carlita, her face deathly pale and her eyes wide open in terror, stood in the middle of a small clearing with her back to the T-Rex.

The T-Rex looked ahead. It didn't move either.

Mitch quickly set Macy down. He leaned out of the brush to follow Carlita's gaze. His heart nearly stopped.

Thirty feet in front of Carlita stood another T-Rex, standing over its kill. Its ferocious face seemed to frown on the intrusion.

Both T-Rexes roared out a challenge. They charged.

Mitch watched in horror as Carlita stood between two furious T-Rexes, both coming right at her.

Macy, who had moved up next to him so she could see what was going on, let out a blood-curdling scream.

WITH a boost from Jeff, Wayne scrambled up the tree and perched high up in the branches.

"What do you see?" Jeff called up, feeling a sense of foreboding growing in his mind.

"I can see the lake," Wayne yelled enthusiastically. "It's only a little ways away."

"Which direction?" Riley asked.

Wayne pointed and Jeff took a bearing on the sun, although he wasn't sure it would do any good. "Okay," he said, "as long as we keep heading that way, we should be able to find it."

"Shhh," Riley said, spinning around. "Do you hear that?"

Cocking his head, Jeff listened. "No, what was it?"

"I'm not sure, but it almost sounded like a girl screaming."

A grave fear shot through Jeff that one of the girls was in serious trouble.

Wayne, now halfway to the ground, said, "It has to be Carlita or Macy."

"Mitch will do everything in his power to keep them safe," Jeff said, not having a lot of confidence in his own words. Would Mitch's efforts be enough? "Could you tell which way it came from?" he asked Riley, realizing they might be fairly close.

"No," Riley said looking around at the trees. "It was really faint. Like it came from all over…like an echo or something."

Jeff put his hands to his mouth and yelled, "*Mitch! Can you hear me? Where are you?*" He held his breath, hoping to hear an answer.

After a few moments with no response, Wayne took a deep breath and let out a loud, high-pitched scream that would have done any girl proud.

Jeff covered his ears.

When Wayne finished, Riley said, "If they didn't hear that, they aren't going to hear anything."

"Shhh," Jeff said, listening for a return call.

Nothing but the subdued sounds of the forest came through the bushes. It was as if whatever animals lived in the area were still fearful of being found by the T-Rex and were keeping a low, quiet profile.

Disappointed and growing worried about Mitch and the girls, Jeff said, "We can't walk around in circles looking for them. Let's get to the lake and follow it back to where we got separated. Hopefully, Mitch will be there waiting for us. Then we can go home."

Jeff took the lead, heading in the direction Wayne had pointed out.

Riley brought up the rear.

The brush grew thicker and thicker. At times, Jeff had to chop his way through with the machete. When one arm got tired, he would switch to the other.

He finally stopped. "It's going to take me forever to hack through this stuff and we haven't come that far." Sweat dripped off his nose. He wiped at his face with his hand. "We need to go back and find another way around. Maybe there's a game trail or something we can follow."

Riley and Wayne, their shirts and hair also dripping wet, headed back with him in the opposite direction.

IN horror, Mitch watched the unfolding events from his hidden position in the bushes.

As the two T-Rexes charged each other, Carlita ran off to the side, right toward Mitch and Macy. Wide-eyed, white-faced, and shaking with fear, she slid to a stop in front of Mitch. "I want to go home, *right now*," she demanded.

Mitch winced. "We can't. We need Riley and his computer." He reached out to take her arm. "Come on, we need to get out of here while those two are occupied."

She yanked her arm away. Her nostrils flared. Her eyes narrowed to slits. "Don't touch me. You're the one responsible for me and Macy being here. Come on, Macy, let's go." She shoved her way past Mitch.

"I can't walk," Macy said, looking over her shoulder at the two dinos now circling, grunting, and growling, as if they were calling each other bad names.

The dinos seemed to be sizing each other up, calculating the chance of winning the fight before another clash.

Mitch wasn't sure why Carlita was putting all the blame on him, but he decided this wasn't the time to deal with it. He wiggled his fingers at Macy in a come-here gesture. "I'll carry you again." He switched his rifle to his left hand and held out his right arm. Bending over a little bit, he nodded for Macy to lay across his shoulder.

After a last fearful look at the dueling dinos still screaming insults at each other, she took two hopping steps and let him pick her up in a fireman's carry.

Carlita took off down the trail at a fast pace, forcing Mitch to hurry or risk losing sight of her.

The T-Rexes started round two.

Mitch hoped they would remain so busy, they wouldn't notice three puny humans running away.

CHAPTER 21

TERRY reached the creek. Dejected and more than a little bit worried, he sat on a rock and contemplated the situation.

Riley and his group weren't to be seen.

Terry kept telling himself that they were still in the area, that they hadn't gone home yet. He couldn't allow himself to believe anything else or he might as well lay down and die, right here and now.

Well, no, he wasn't that stupid. If he had been left here alone, he would probably die in the first week. He might have prevented that if he had brought his backpack full of gear. As it stood now, all he had in his pockets were his key chain with two keys and a pair of nail clippers, his wallet with money and credit cards, and his belt. No knife, no matches, not even an extra shirt or jacket.

He looked up at the sky. He couldn't see the sun because the hills and vegetation surrounded him, but judging by the quality of the light, he figured it would be dark in an hour, maybe less.

Sighing he stood up, careful not to bump his broken arm or ribs. "I need to find somewhere to spend the night." His words sounded strange against the backdrop of jungle sounds coming from all around him.

He scanned the surrounding area and studied the geological makeup of the ground. The few rocks looked like granite, but then again, he couldn't tell the difference between granite, schist, and limestone. He did remember something about sandstone containing more caves than other types of rocks, something about how it eroded faster.

So far, he hadn't seen any kind of shelter, but then again,

he hadn't been looking for a place to spend the night. He recalled seeing a lot of rocks on his path. Thinking he might get lucky and stumble onto a cave or a place to hide under large rocks, he took a drink of water and started following the creek back upstream.

AS the sounds of the T-Rex fight receded, Mitch's breathing became labored. The off-and-on running with a full pack would've been bad enough, but with Macy's added weight, he ran out of reserves fast. Despite his best effort, he lost sight of Carlita after the first hundred or so yards. Stopping momentarily, he filled his lungs. "*Carlita*," he bellowed, his voice loud in spite of his condition. "Wait for us." He knew yelling was a risk. He only hoped the T-Rexes were so busy with each other that they would ignore his call.

Mitch forced his legs to move again. He stumbled on, but grew so tired that his rhythm got off-balance, causing him to run with a jarring gate. Stumbling, he almost fell. He began using his rifle like a walking stick to keep himself erect.

"Ooof," Macy's breath shot out as his shoulder punched her in the gut. "Hey, take it easy, Mitch. I'm sure if she gets too far ahead, she'll come back for us."

Legs shaking, he set Macy on the ground. Slipping his pack off, he sank to his knees. He lowered his rifle to the ground, then fell back on his pack. Arms sprawled out, sides heaving, he tried to catch his breath. Sweat ran out of his soaked hair and streamed down his face. Gasping, he said, "She'd better come back...I have all the food."

AS Jeff and his brothers headed back the way they had come, a jolting crash and a loud growl behind him made Jeff glad they had turned around. He quickened his pace, keeping up with his brothers, who must have heard the noises, too.

Reaching an area where the brush seemed to be less dense, Jeff said, "Okay, from here, let's head to the right. We'll keep aiming toward the water and, sooner or later, we'll have to find some way to get through."

Letting Riley lead this time, Jeff brought up the rear. Keeping an eye out for anything that might sneak up on them, he almost missed the trail. "Hey, Riley, Wayne," he called out, "look at this trail. I think it heads toward the water." In the growing heat, they had emptied their small canteens again.

"Water," Wayne drawled out, collapsing to the ground at Jeff's feet. "I would love a drink of water."

"We'll get you a drink as soon as we can," Riley said, concern showing clearly on his face. "We need to find some water as soon as possible," he said to Jeff. "We're all getting dehydrated in this heat."

"I know," Jeff said. "I'm thirsty, too." Reaching down, he pulled Wayne to his feet. "Come on, let's go get a drink at the lake."

"Drink, yeah, water," Wayne muttered as he stumbled onto the trail.

Jeff tripped along behind Wayne, making sure his scrawny little brother didn't drop on the path and get left behind.

AS Mitch lay on his backpack, still trying to catch his breath, a crash in the bushes to the right side of the trail interrupted his rest. He took his arms out of the straps, rolled off his pack, and swept up his rifle. Remaining on his knees, he brought the rifle to his shoulder and clicked the safety off. "Get behind me, Macy. And if I tell you to, run like hell."

She moaned in fear, but hobbled on her bad foot to get behind him.

The crashing grew louder and constant, like something forcing its way through the brush.

Mitch caught the barest glimpse of movement and instantly centered his sights on the spot. Tightening his finger on the trigger, he took a deep breath and slowly let it out in anticipation of firing.

As Carlita burst from the bush, Mitch screamed, "What the hell!" With shaking hands, he put the safety on and lowered the rifle. "What are you doin', girl? I just about shot you."

She glared at him. "For your information, I was evading another dinosaur. It was on the trail. I had to force my way through the bushes to escape."

Getting to his feet, Mitch looked at her sweats, torn and covered with dirt.

Her black hair, normally sleek and shiny, was tangled and full of twigs and leaves. Branches had slapped against her face, leaving angry red welts and open cuts. One large cut, high on her forehead, looked like it would need stitches. Blood ran down her face along the outer edge of her left eye and continued down to her chin. Her right eye was puffy and turning black. She looked like she'd been in a fight or a car wreck.

Mitch looked up the trail in the direction where she'd gone earlier. "Do you think the dinosaur is coming this way?"

She put her hands on her hips. "How the hell should I know? I didn't stop long enough to ask it which direction it was going."

"Oookay," he replied, thinking he needed to tread carefully or risk really pissing her off. "Did you happen to notice what kind of dinosaur it was?"

"I don't know. I think it was one of those raptor-thingers." She moved to Macy's side.

Mitch's mind grappled with the thought of tangling with a group of raptors. All he knew of raptors was what he'd seen on the old movie *Jurassic Park* he and Jeff had watched a few years back. In the movie, these creatures had been portrayed as sneaky, efficient killers. They hunted in packs and were smart enough to plan ahead.

Before they had actually taken this trip through time, Mitch hadn't been sure the time machine would really work, but he had imagined such an adventure would be fun and exciting. The reality of it was proving to be a hell of a lot scarier than anything he could have thought up himself. With T-Rexes and raptors running loose, there was no way he could indefinitely protect the girls from harm. "I think we need to hurry back to the brook where we were before the stampede. Hopefully, Jeff, Riley, and Wayne are there waiting, and we can go home."

"Then let's go," Carlita said, impatiently holding her hands on her hips.

Mitch's shoulders slumped. "The problem is, I don't think I can carry Macy anymore. I just don't have anything left...I'm sorry." Knowing he was letting them down, he kept his eyes on the ground, unable to look at either of them.

"Fine," Carlita barked. "You stay here. I'll help her." She slid her arm around Macy's waist. "Macy, put your arm over my shoulder and lean on me. We won't be able to go very fast, but at least we'll be moving."

With Macy hobbling along beside her, Carlita started down the path without a backward glance.

Mitch couldn't believe Carlita's nerve to leave him behind like that. *Hell, she doesn't have food or any way to make a fire or anything.* Slinging his pack on his back, he sighed and dug deep within himself, looking for reserves of energy that he knew were getting dangerously low. On weak, shaky legs, he followed after them.

CHAPTER 22

TERRY barely covered a quarter of a mile before he had to stop and take a break. After getting a drink, he sat down next to the creek.

A strange crunching noise came from the brush to the east of him. The noise stopped, replaced by a low hum that sounded almost like a cat purring, only ten times louder and much lower in pitch.

Knowing it couldn't be a cat because they supposedly didn't exist in this era, Terry got up and walked toward the brush out of curiosity. Finding a narrow path through the brush, he moved as quietly as possible.

A small dinosaur, about two feet tall with a blood-stained face, ran by, upright on its rear feet and its front legs holding a chunk of red meat.

I wonder what it's been eating? Terry thought as he crept forward a little more.

Suddenly, a large open area appeared in front of him. One of the dinosaurs that had stampeded earlier lay dead on the ground. Lying next to it was the source of the noise Terry had heard: a T-Rex.

Terry's mouth dropped open in shock.

With its eyes closed, the T-Rex's head lay on top of the dead dinosaur's body.

Terry took a moment to figure out that the T-Rex had eaten its fill and was now either resting or asleep.

The purring noise stopped as the T-Rex repositioned its head. With a loud moan, the T-Rex relaxed and the purring started again.

Could the T-Rex be a distant relative of the modern cat?

Terry wondered. After all, modern science could only do so much with bones. *Who's to say the scientists of our modern era don't make mistakes?*

Backing away cautiously, Terry retraced his steps to the creek and continued upstream, all the while keeping his eyes open for a safe place to spend the night.

OSBORNE had been following Terry since Terry had awakened from unconsciousness and made his way back to the creek. Stealthily, he had stayed well behind Terry by following his footprints.

Now, Osborne hid on the other side of the clearing where Terry had studied the resting T-Rex.

Osborne had a good view of the dino's mouth, including its huge teeth. He was glad he had the grenade launcher on his rifle because he doubted that anything short of an elephant gun would stop something as big as this creature.

Osborne moved on to stay up with Terry, which wasn't difficult, being that Terry seemed to be injured and was moving slowly. Bored and hungry, Osborne wished Terry would stop long enough for Osborne to get something to eat.

At least, it would be dark soon. Terry would have to settle in for the night.

At that point, Osborne could eat and relax until morning. As he made his way quietly along the trail, he thought back to the sleeping T-Rex. It gave him the chills. He suspected the creature wouldn't be hunting tonight, but he hoped there weren't any others out looking for a meal. He wouldn't want to face one of them in the light of day, let alone in the dark of night.

JEFF lifted his hand and wiped the sweat out of his eyes.

The trail they had been following wove through the brush heading in the general direction of the lake. The vegetation grew thicker the further they went. The trail resembled a tunnel made out of bushes. Other, smaller trails led off from the larger trail, but Jeff stayed on the main trail since it was heading in the direction of the lake.

Every time Jeff heard a grunt, growl, or other loud noise in the bushes, he jumped. In the growing darkness, and with their fatigue and thirst, there was no way they could outrun a dinosaur if one showed itself to them now. It surprised him that they still had enough energy to keep going.

The trail turned.

Jeff saw water ahead. Quickening his pace, he speed-walked through the last hundred feet of brush. Coming out on a stretch of shoreline, he glanced to his left and right. Making sure there were no dinosaurs in sight, he hurried to the water's edge, plopped down on his knees, and began taking slow sips. He'd learned the lesson from Riley about drinking too much too fast.

When the three of them had their fill, Jeff stood up and looked around. "It'll be dark soon. We need to find a place to spend the night."

"I'm not real comfortable with that," Wayne said.

"Me neither," Jeff retorted, "but we don't have an option." They couldn't leave without Mitch and the girls. Or could they? He looked at Riley's computer.

"I don't want to sleep here," Wayne whined. "This place is scary enough in daylight when you can see."

Jeff secretly agreed with him. He wasn't looking forward to spending a night in this strange land, not knowing what kind of animals would be roaming around in the darkness. "Riley, what would happen if we went home and came back tomorrow? Would we end up in the same place and at the same time as now?"

In the dimming light. Riley's eyes darkened with anger. "We're *not* leaving without the others." He held his laptop tighter to his chest, as if he thought Jeff might try to take it from him.

"We're going to spend the night away from them

anyway," Jeff explained. "We might as well be comfortable and safe."

"*No*," Riley shot out as he jumped up and moved a few feet away. "I can't guarantee we'll come back to this exact time and place. I'm not going to take the chance of leaving them here permanently."

Deep down, Jeff knew Riley was right. He couldn't imagine leaving his friends stranded here forever. They had all come together, and they would all have to return together. He'd just have to find a way to deal with Wayne's fears and his own fears. "Okay, okay. In that case, we'd better start looking for a safe place to spend the night."

"What about up a tree?" Wayne asked.

Jeff pictured them all sleeping on a tree branch fifty feet up in the air. "I think we'd be better off on the ground. I'd hate for any of us to roll over in our sleep and fall out of the tree."

"We'll tie ourselves to a limb so we can't fall," Wayne suggested eagerly, his eyes scanning the surrounding area for a tree.

"I'm with Wayne on this one," Riley said. "I think we'd be much safer up off of the ground where nothing can come along and eat us."

"Fine," Jeff blurted. "Let's see if we can find a tall tree." He wondered if Mitch and the girls were even alive, and how the girls would manage through the blackness of the night. A shiver rode down his spine at the thought of the long hours they would all be apart and, worse, what they might find in the morning.

CHAPTER 23

AFTER what seemed like an endless hike behind the two girls, Mitch collapsed on the ground next to them. They all dripped with sweat and panted heavily.

They sat under a lone pine tree in a small clearing about a hundred feet across of mostly bare dirt. Short grass and a few bushes cropped up here and there. They had a clear line of sight in case anything showed up.

"It's going to get dark soon," he said. "I don't think we're going to make it back tonight."

Macy sat up straight. "We aren't going to spend the night here, are we?"

"We don't have much of a choice," he replied, not crazy about it either. He just hoped they were far enough from the T-Rexes and the raptors to be safe.

"I'm sorry," Macy said sharply, shaking her head, "I refuse to sleep in the dirt. Who knows what will crawl on us in the dark?"

"It's okay," Carlita reassured her. "I'm sure Mitch can start a fire. We can take turns keeping watch so nothing gets us." She glared at Mitch as if daring him to challenge her.

Wisely, he said, "Sure, no problem."

Macy suddenly shot a concerned look at Carlita. "Your mom will be worried about us. We were supposed to sleep at your house tonight."

"No, she won't," Carlita snapped. "She'll probably come home late with her new boyfriend and won't even notice we aren't there. If she sees us gone, she'll think we're at your house."

Mitch felt bad about Carlita's changing home life, but he

had other things to hold his attention right now. He leaned his rifle against the nearby tree and slipped off his pack. Unzipping one of the outer pockets, he reached in and pulled out a Bic lighter and a pill bottle. Setting these on the ground, he started gathering kindling from the base of a pine tree.

While he gathered the small sticks and twigs, he kept a wary eye on the surroundings. He listened carefully to the noises around them. He didn't want a T-Rex or other creature sneaking up on him while he was occupied. Once he had enough kindling, he gathered larger pieces of wood until he had a pile large enough to last all night, and then some. He wanted to make sure they didn't run short and have the fire go out, leaving them in the dark.

While he gathered the wood, Carlita and Macy picked up the rocks to make the fire ring. They put them in a circle on a large patch of bare dirt. When he was ready to start the fire, Mitch opened the pill bottle and took out a cotton ball. Fluffing it up, he set it on the ground and piled kindling on top of it. Seeing the skeptical looks on the girls' faces, he said, "The cotton is soaked with petroleum jelly. It acts like an accelerant. It'll burn for at least two or three minutes, plenty long enough to get the kindling burning, even if the wood is wet."

"Pretty smart," Carlita said softly, seeming more relaxed and accepting of the situation. "Where'd you learn that?"

"Boy Scouts." He held his hand up in the Boy Scout salute. "Like the motto says, 'Be Prepared.'"

"I'm glad you are," Macy said with a hint of admiration in her voice. "Otherwise, we'd be cold and scared all night." She wrapped her arms around her chest and shivered, as if the thought of not having a fire to light up the night was the worst thing that could happen to them.

Sensing Carlita's anger had diminished, Mitch said, "And you don't have to worry about anything crawling on you, I brought a tent for us to sleep in."

Macy let out a little squeal of delight. "Oh, Mitch, thank you. You're my hero."

Carlita rolled her eyes at Macy's theatrical antics. "The tent will be nice, but I hope you also brought some food along. I'm starving."

"Not to worry, Ladies, once I get the fire going, I'll whip up a meal better than anything you could eat at home."

"Yeah, right," Macy said as she watched him light the cotton ball. "I doubt if I'll like anything you can make out here, unless you have a couple of Big Macs in your pack, that is." She licked her lips.

He laughed. The thought of a big, juicy hamburger sounded pretty good to him, too. "You'd be surprised at what I have in there. How does beef stroganoff with noodles and corn sound?"

"You really have that?" Macy asked wide-eyed.

"You bet." He winked at her. "I even have blueberry cheesecake for dessert."

"You've got to be kidding me," Carlita said, doubt written all over her face.

"Nope, you'd be amazed at what kind of freeze-dried food is available nowadays."

Carlita rolled her eyes.

Macy giggled in delight.

As the kindling caught fire, Mitch added larger and larger pieces of wood until he had a stable fire going. Looking at the sky, he said, "It's gonna get dark before too long, so before I cook dinner, I want to set up the tent."

AS the sun lowered beneath the horizon, Jeff knew it would be dark before long. He pointed to a tall pine down the shoreline. "Let's try that one."

On closer inspection, the tree, probably a redwood, looked pretty good as far as having thick, heavy branches sprouting out of the middle of it. The problem was that they couldn't climb it, being branch-free near the ground. Jeff stared up at the closest branch, a good twenty feet above his head. "Great, now what?"

"Maybe you can boost me up," Wayne said.

"And then what?" Jeff demanded.

"Then I'll tie off a rope and you can climb up," Wayne replied smugly.

"Do you have a rope?" Jeff asked.

Wayne's eyes darted around. "No, but we can probably find some vines or something we can use." He wandered off.

"What a dweeb," Jeff muttered.

"He's just trying to help," Riley said with irritation.

Jeff ignored the comment. "We either need to find another tree or come up with another plan." He yelled, "Wayne, get back here. It's too dark to go wandering around by yourself."

"Hey," Wayne called out, "I think I found a place to stay."

Jeff and Riley hurried to the spot.

A giant tree had fallen in the recent past and, as luck would have it, it had fallen across two large, square-sided boulders that sat adjacent to each other, forming a V. The tree trunk, at least ten feet in diameter, completely covered the back half of the V and acted as a roof. Branches, still covered with clumps of dead needles, hid most of the front area. The opening of the V stretched ten feet across with the roofed area going back twenty feet deep. The tree sat six inches above Jeff's head from the entrance to the back, just enough room for him to stand up.

"If we build a fire here," Wayne said, standing in the mouth of the V, "it should scare away anything that comes around in the dark."

"It looks good to me," Riley said, moving in and sitting with his back against the rock.

Jeff had to agree that it was as good a spot as they were going to find. He swung his pack off. "We need lots of wood. You two start gathering that. I'll get a fire going."

ALONG his trail, Terry couldn't find a place that even remotely looked like a safe location to spend the night. He grew more and more worried that it would get too dark to see. He'd been hoping for a cave or an overhanging rock, but so far, the best bet for hiding was a pine tree with very low branches that he could crawl under. After closer inspection, though, he decided not to go with the pine tree because of the holes in the dirt close to the base of the tree. He didn't know what might be living in the holes, and didn't want to find out.

Continuing his search in the growing darkness, he came upon a clump of bushes with softball-sized cotton-like clusters growing on them. He figure that a bunch of these branches could be used as padding underneath him for a mattress, as well as a kind of blanket to keep him warm if it got cold later. Once he found a shelter, he would come back and pick some of the branches.

Walking farther from the creek, he wandered aimlessly, half-heartedly giving up on finding a good place, when he saw a tree that had fallen and gotten caught in the branches of another tree, leaving the trunk off the ground. This would have worked, but he had wanted something a little more protected. He wanted a barrier strong and solid behind him.

Feeling like a total failure, he turned and headed back toward the creek. There, at least, he'd have access to water. If anything, he wouldn't die of thirst.

In the growing twilight and coming from a different direction, he got a different view of the jungle, something he hadn't seen before: a jumble of rocks with a hollowed-out spot. Not wanting to let himself get too optimistic, he quelled the excitement coursing through his body as he hurried closer to take a better look.

The rock pile turned out to be even better than he'd hoped for. The opening gave him just enough room to crawl inside and lay down. From what he could tell, there were no signs that this spot was being used by any kind of animal. No droppings, no nests, no food leftovers. The place sat close to the cottony-looking bushes, too.

Terry hurried back to the bushes as quickly as his injuries would allow. He bent the branches and smashed them with his feet. Using this method, he loosened the short roots just enough to pull them out with his one good arm.

He made two quick trips before it got to dark to see. After that, he feared he'd get turned around in the dark and not find his way back to his humble shelter.

CHAPTER 24

OPENING the main compartment of his pack, Mitch reached in and pulled out a long, skinny bundle. It didn't take more than five minutes, and he had a three-person tent ready to go about ten feet from the fire.

"What about blankets?" Macy asked, her brows raised in doubt.

Mitch dipped into his pack again. This time, he pulled out two small bundles. He held one in each hand. "Survival blankets, made from wool, very warm. Unfortunately, I only have two, so the two of you can use them and I'll use my jacket." He threw one of the bundles to each of them. "If you'll make the beds, I'll start dinner." He knew laying out two blankets wouldn't take the girls very long, but he hoped that giving them something to do would take their minds off the last few hours and the night still to come.

He heard the murmur of the girl's voices from the tent as they made up the beds. Feeling optimistic about the upcoming night, he pulled several packages out of his pack and started their dinner.

One of the packages contained a set of two pots for boiling water and two frying pans that doubled as lids for the pots. Pouring a little water into both pots from one of his two canteens, he set them on the edge of the fire to heat up. Next, he took out two stainless-steel plates and utensils. When he'd packed, he hadn't known the girls would be coming on the trip, so he'd only brought a set for himself and an extra one in case Jeff or one of his brothers needed it.

He decided to let the girls eat first. Then, he'd clean a set and eat his dinner.

The girls came out of the tent and started walking away from camp with Carlita helping Macy limp along.

"Whoa, wait a minute. Where ya going?" Mitch asked, coming to his feet in alarm.

"To the bathroom," Carlita called over her shoulder without missing a step.

"Stop right there," he bellowed. "That bush is plenty far enough."

They stopped and turned around.

Macy said, "But, Mitch–"

"But nothing, Macy." He put his hands on his hips defiantly. "I want you where I can get to you fast if a dinosaur shows up."

"Mitch, we need our privacy," Carlita retorted.

He shook his head. "I'm sorry, Carlita. You're going to have to sacrifice privacy for safety. I promise I won't look or come any closer."

Macy stared at the thin, almost leafless four-foot-tall bush next to her. "This isn't big enough to hide behind. I'd rather go over there." She pointed to the thicker brush fifty feet away on the outskirts of their little clearing.

"No way. Who knows what might be lurking in there?" Before either one could argue, he sternly added, "I'm not budging on this. You can go there or not at all."

Carlita's face contorted with rage. "That's a bunch of bull, Mitch. We'll go where we want." She took Macy by the arm, but her eyes were locked on Mitch. "I don't need his permission, and if he thinks he can tell me where to go, he's sadly mistaken." She turned the two of them around and, without a backward glance, headed for the brush.

E.T. chuckled to himself. He'd been hiding in the bushes behind Mitch, close enough to overhear most of the conversation. Now, he had names to go with the faces. He also picked up a fair idea of their personalities and capabilities.

It hadn't taken long to realize that Mitch was highly competent and most likely capable of keeping the two girls safe on his own. Mitch looked too young to have been in the military, but he would fit right in by nature.

E.T. surmised that Mitch and Macy were boyfriend and girlfriend, and Carlita was the girlfriend of Riley's older brother Jeff.

Of the two girls, he worried more about Macy. She seemed more fragile and prissy than Carlita, who'd shown her bravery by facing the two T-Rexes earlier and now confronting Mitch.

Feeling like Mitch would keep everything generally under control, E.T. eased out of his hiding spot and quietly moved back to find a place for the night. He wanted to be close enough that he could get to them in a hurry, but far enough that if Mitch went out for wood, he wouldn't stumble on E.T.'s camp.

THE ground under the fallen tree was covered with pine needles and small twigs. Jeff pulled out his flashlight to see what he was doing as he pushed the debris to the side with his foot, clearing an area big enough for the three of them to sleep in. He tried using his hands to scoop out a pit for the fire, but the ground was packed too hard. He needed a tool to dig it out.

Riley and Wayne came back with their first load of wood and dumped it near one of the rocks.

"It's getting too dark to see what we're doing," Riley stated as he went to his backpack. He rummaged around and pulled out a flashlight. Clicking it on, he nodded to Wayne. Wordlessly, they went in search of more wood.

Jeff looked at the machete, now leaning against the rock near the entrance. *No, I hadn't better. Mitch will be pissed if I dig a hole with it and dull the blade.* Instead, he pulled a piece of wood out of the pile and used it to scrape at the floor. After breaking through the top layer of dirt, the digging got easier. He cleared an area about two feet across and a foot deep, scattering the dirt in a half circle on the back side of the pit for them to lay on. By the time he was done, Riley and Wayne were back with more wood.

After dumping his load, Wayne plopped onto the ground.

"What do you think you're doing?" Jeff asked.

Wayne shrugged his shoulders as if it was obvious. "Resting."

"You can rest later. Get your butt out there and help Riley get more wood." Jeff knew he sounded harsh after the hard day they had experienced, but this was important.

Wayne looked at the pile of wood. "That should be plenty, don't you think, Riley?"

"Jeff's right, we need more." Riley let out a sigh, seeming plenty exhausted himself. "I don't want to run out in the middle of the night."

"Aw, come on," Wayne whined. "I'm tired and hungry."

"Wayne," Jeff said sternly, "get out there and help Riley or I'll make you sleep outside. And I won't let you eat dinner." It sounded lame, but it was all Jeff could come up with at the moment. It wasn't like he could threaten to tell Mom that Wayne wasn't cooperating.

Wayne's lower lip curled into a pout. He lowered his head to his hands and started crying.

"Jeez," Jeff blurted, shaking his head in disgust.

"Give him a break," Riley said, sitting down and putting an arm around Wayne's shoulders.

"*No!*" Jeff yelled, startling both of them. "He's just as responsible for us being here as any of the rest of us, so he can just cut the poor-tired-baby routine and do his part."

"I'm scared," Wayne shot back, tears running down his face. "And I want to go home."

"Yeah, well that's too bad," Jeff said as he walked to the entrance of their little shelter. "I am, too, but there are things we need to do if we want to get through the night alive. Come on, I'll go with you to get more wood. Once we're done, we can eat dinner." He picked up his flashlight and looked at them expectantly. "Well, you coming or what?"

"Give me a minute, okay?" Riley leaned down and

whispered in Wayne's ear.

Wayne sniffed and answered back.

After a short, personal conversation, Wayne nodded his head and Riley smiled. Wiping his eyes, Wayne stood up. "I'm sorry, Jeff. I just got really scared and homesick for a minute."

Feeling like an ass for being so hard on Wayne, Jeff said, "It's okay. I'm sorry, too. I shouldn't have yelled at you like that."

A distant growl somewhere in the trees behind them cut the touchy-feely moment off.

Grabbing his flashlight, Riley headed out. "Let's get our wood and get back before whatever that is gets closer."

CHAPTER 25

TERRY stuffed the fluffy branches into the opening of his rock shelter. As he crawled inside, he pushed some of them down to act as padding to lay on. The others, he pulled over himself like a blanket. He stuck his feet in first, so his head lay close to the opening. He could easily look out if he heard strange noises.

The wind picked up and sounded like white noise on a T.V., lulling Terry into a state of sleepiness. Lying on his back, he looked up at the little bit of sky he could see above him. There were no clouds, just more stars than he'd ever seen. Of course, it wasn't like he'd ever paid attention to the stars back home. If he happened to be out at night, he had more important things to do than gaze up at the stars like an idiot. He had to admit though, the stars tonight were an amazing sight to see. He wondered if they were this bright at home. He doubted it, not unless someone was a long way from all the city lights. Even then, he imagined that all the pollution hanging in the air would affect how the stars appeared.

Other than the sound of the wind through the trees, all was quiet, as if all the animals had gone to sleep as night had fallen. Terry hoped so, but he feared he might not be that lucky. The best he could hope for was to not be found by anything big enough to move the rocks to get to him. A smaller creature he could deal with.

He scooted himself as far into the shelter as possible. His arm and ribs throbbed, but he ignored them. Closing his eyes, he took a deep relaxing breath and drifted off to sleep.

FINALLY, Osborne thought as Terry settled in for the night. Now, he could settle in himself. As he'd been following Terry around, he'd been looking for a likely spot for the night. As it turned out, the best spot showed itself not very far from where Terry made his bed.

Comfortably ensconced in his tent with a full stomach, Osborne knew he probably wouldn't get much sleep. He'd watched Terry break off branches to make his bed. He felt sorry for Terry. *Poor guy. He doesn't know what he is doing. He can't seem to catch a break.*

Osborne chuckled to himself. He knew exactly what that cotton on the branches really was. When it happened, it wasn't going to be fun for Terry.

AFTER Carlita's defiant stance, Mitch angrily watched them head down the trail. He clenched his hands into fists. His breathing and pulse rate sped up. With his anger about to explode, he needed an outlet other than Carlita to release it on. He looked around to no avail.

Suddenly, when the girls were halfway across the clearing, a pack of ten small dinos, about two feet tall, rushed out of the bushes and surrounded them. Cackling similar to modern-day hyenas, the dinos didn't appear to be intimidated by the screams and shooing motions coming from the two girls.

Mitch's first thought was to pick up his gun, but with the girls so close, he didn't dare use it. Still angry, he swept a stout branch off the pile of firewood and charged.

The dinos scattered as he plowed through them, but they weren't quick enough to save two of their numbers from a sudden death at the end of Mitch's make-do weapon.

Carlita and Macy hurried back toward the camp while Mitch chased the remaining dinos down the trail, making sure they were gone for good.

When he returned, he didn't say a word. It wasn't in his nature to rub it in when someone did something wrong. Instead, he went about doing what needed to be done. The fire had burned down to coals, so he added more wood and repositioned the pots of water. He figured the girls had used the bushes closer to camp while he was gone. At least, he hoped they had.

He got a rope out of his pack, slung his rifle across his shoulder, and walked back to the two dinos he'd killed with the stick. Looping the rope around both animals, he drug them away from camp. The last thing they needed tonight was to have dead meat lying near their campsite. That was in invitation to dinner for every meat-eater in the area.

When he returned to camp, Macy wrenched her hands together and softly said, "We're sorry, Mitch. We should have listened to you. Do you forgive us?"

Carlita elbowed her in the ribs. "You might be sorry, Macy, but I'm not. Mitch knows better than to order me around. Until he apologizes, I'm not speaking to him."

Her tone was so cold, he shivered, even though he was on the other side of the fire.

She crossed her arms over her chest and stared at him in expectation of an immediate apology.

Mitch had a tough decision to make. It was either apologize to her and let her have the upper hand, or gather more wood, since it was getting too dark to see. He knew if he caved in and apologized, she would challenge him like this again in the future. He considered what had happened while he put more wood on the fire, and he still came to the same conclusion. He didn't think he'd been wrong insisting that the girls stay close. Therefore, he wasn't about to apologize.

Damn, it's gonna be a long, cold night. He grabbed his flashlight and headed out of camp. He was back in less than ten minutes with a huge armload of wood.

E.T. had barely turned around to find a place for the night when he'd heard the girls screaming. Tightening his grip on his gun, he'd hurried back and watched from behind a bush as Mitch took on a pack of hyena-sized dinosaurs with nothing more than a long stick. He had to admire Mitch. It looked like the young man had everything under control again.

E.T. observed the group for a few more minutes. Seeing that things were in order, he quietly made his way through the brush to find a place for his own campsite. It wasn't long before he was sitting in his tent and eating his dinner. With any luck, he'd be able to get a few uninterrupted hours of sleep before the next catastrophe hit.

CHAPTER 26

IT didn't take long until Jeff, Riley, and Wayne had enough wood piled up to satisfy Jeff's expectations for the night. Jeff quickly built a roaring fire, which almost caught the tree above them ablaze. Luckily, they put it out before it got out of hand.

Jeff was now glad he'd brought a backpack, but wished he'd thrown in more food...lots more food. The peanut-butter-and-honey sandwich, a Ziploc baggie of potato chips, and a can of Vienna Sausages wouldn't go very far toward feeding all three of them. "We'll have to split this three ways," he said as he held out the food.

Riley shook his head, smiled, and opened his backpack. "I had a feeling we might need extra food," he explained. He laid a towel on the ground and started pulling out the food.

Jeff was shocked to see Riley had brought the whole jar of peanut butter, a bottle of honey, a slightly smashed loaf of white bread, three cans of Kippered snacks, three individual serving packs of chocolate pudding, a package of beef jerky, and a bag of Captain Crunch cereal.

"That's for breakfast," Riley said. He'd even brought plastic utensils, paper towels, and a bag for their garbage.

Jeff's stomach growled at the sight of it. "Wow, I'm impressed."

Wayne grabbed the bread and proceeded to make a sandwich. "Me, too. Let's eat."

Jeff took a bite of his pre-made sandwich. "I bet Mitch and the girls aren't eating this good," he said around a mouthful of food.

Wayne took a huge bite of his sandwich and rolled his

eyes in mock ecstasy. "They don't know what they're missing."

"I'm sure Mitch will come up with something for them to eat," Riley said. "Heck, he'll probably shoot a dinosaur so they can have steaks."

"He'll probably root around and find wild carrots and potatoes, too," Jeff added with a smile.

Wayne hurriedly swallowed so he could get in on the game. "I'll bet they have a salad made from all-natural ingredients." He giggled.

Jeff mused that the only food *not* natural in the world at this moment in time, with the exception of Mitch's grub, was sitting right here in front of them.

He looked around at their little shelter. He thought they'd done pretty well, considering the circumstances. They had a roof over their heads in the form of a tree trunk, two walls in the shape of a V, walls of rock that would protect them from attacks on the back and sides. The fire at the mouth of the V would keep anything dangerous at bay…he hoped.

After finishing their dinner, they lay down next to each with their backpacks as pillows.

Jeff closed his eyes and sighed. W*e're gonna be okay,* he thought as he drifted off to sleep.

TAYLOR sat snuggly in his tent just up the beach from Riley and his brothers. He'd followed them until he was sure they were settled in. Then, he'd found a spot for his tent in the bushes, a place hard to see in the light of day. Even if Riley or someone else came wandering around at night, there was no way they would see it.

He ate his dinner consisting of MREs, washed down with water. *This isn't so bad,* he thought as he pulled out a paperback book and lay back on his sleeping bag.

A crash in the jungle, followed by a deep, menacing growl, sent chills over his entire body. He sat up and listened for more noises. When he heard nothing, he opened the book.

His hands shook slightly.

He couldn't concentrate. After five minutes of staring at the same page, he put the book away. He didn't know if his fear came from worrying about the outcome of the mission or because of what was roaming around out there in the dark. Maybe a little of both.

MITCH'S freeze-dried gourmet dinner was a big hit with Macy, who *oohed* and *awwed* throughout the meal as if she was eating in a fancy restaurant in N.Y.C.

It earned him a polite, "Thank you," from Carlita, but no more. In fact, as soon as Carlita was done eating, she told Macy she was tired. She went to the tent without saying a word to Mitch.

He cleaned her plate and utensils, then ate his dinner as he stared gloomily into the fire. Halfway through his meal, something big crashed through the bushes just beyond the clearing. Mitch held his rifle at the ready and waited, but heard nothing more.

From that point onward, he kept his eyes averted from the fire so he wouldn't ruin his night vision. His ears became attuned to the sounds of the night, and he knew he'd rely more on his ears than his eyes to warn him of approaching dangers during what promised to be a long night ahead.

"I'm ready to go to sleep now," Macy said after a long tense silence.

Not sure if he'd be welcomed to sleep in the tent with them, Mitch decided to sleep outside. After helping Macy to the tent, he returned to the fire. After all, someone had to keep watch, and it was kind of hard to see what was going on around him if he was cooped up inside a tent. With the mild temperature, he didn't need the fire, but it was comforting, and he knew it would keep most, if not all, the animals away.

Sitting on the ground with his back to the fire and his rifle lying next to him, he started fashioning a crutch for Macy out of a forked tree limb. While he worked, he wondered how

Jeff, Riley, and Wayne were doing. He'd been concerned about them ever since they'd split up.

Jeff wasn't an outdoors type of guy. Neither were the two boys. They each had brought a backpack, but he hadn't thought to ask them what they had in them. For all he knew, Jeff had brought a book or a handheld video game…maybe a jacket. Jeff hadn't believed that this trip was for real, so he probably hadn't brought much at all.

Riley, on the other hand, had probably brought more items conducive to surviving a night in this world. After all, Riley knew they would really be coming here. He and Wayne had made a previous trip. They had an idea of what it would be like.

Mitch felt sure they would have brought at least a change of clothes and some food.

Thinking back, he was glad he'd brought all the gear he had prepared in his pack. Although he hadn't been sure they would really come to this world, the baby Triceratops gave it away. Where else could it have come from? As crazy as it had sounded when Riley told them how the dino had gotten into their house, Mitch had believed that it was the only thing that made sense.

Mitch knew there was no middle ground with him. Either he believed in something or he didn't. Everything was right or wrong, good or bad, black or white. He saw no room in his life for gray. He'd been brought up to stand up for what he believed and to take responsibility for his actions.

His dad had impressed upon him at an early age that he wouldn't tolerate any wishy-washy excuses. When Mitch did a half-assed job on his chores, he got a tongue lashing and another chance to do the job right. If the job didn't meet his dad's approval the second time around, he got a belt across his backside and another chance to do the job. It hadn't taken him long to realize he was better off doing the job right in the first place.

He missed his parents now, wondering if they were missing him. He quickly shook off those concerns, knowing he had more important matters to face at the moment.

Thinking back on his inability to accept gray areas, he

realized that sometimes, like tonight, this attribute worked against him. If he hadn't been so insistent about Carlita and Macy staying close to camp, Carlita wouldn't be mad at him.

Well, Carlita had claimed earlier that he was responsible for them, and he was. Therefore, he wasn't about to let them go wandering around unprotected. He had a job to do and he was going to make damn sure he did it right the first time around.

He looked out into the blackness of his surroundings. In this world, there didn't seem to be many second chances.

CHAPTER 27

JEFF lay on the grass. The blue sky was a perfect backdrop for Carlita, who was bending over him smiling. She pulled a water pistol from behind her back and aimed it at his face. Instead of pulling the trigger, she gently squeezed it until a big, fat drop of water hung on the end of the gun. His eyes stared at it in fascination, waiting for it to fall. When it did, it hit him on the forehead with a wet plop. He felt the water run off the side of his face. Another drop fell. Then another and another until so many were falling that he had to close his eyes.

"Jeff. Jeff, wake up," Carlita said, but in Riley's voice.

Jeff opened his eyes and quickly came wide awake on the ground.

It was still dark outside. Water dripped from the fallen tree that formed a roof above him. Water soaked everything.

"What's happening?" he asked in confusion.

"It's raining," Riley said as he pulled his jacket over his head like an umbrella. A waterproof flashlight, sitting on the ground next to him, provided just enough light to see. He sat hunched over his laptop, shielding it from the rain with his body.

Jeff sat up and noticed the fire was now a lost cause, the fire pit having filled with water. He looked at his watch: *2:34*. They still had roughly four hours until daylight. Not good. Not good at all.

"Jeff, come over here," Wayne said from the back of the shelter.

Wayne knelt in the v-shaped corner with a small keychain

flashlight.

Crawling toward Wayne, Jeff saw an area that was completely dry. The largest part of the tree trunk had formed a protective waterproof barrier where the two rocks came together.

Jeff returned to his sleeping area to get his things. "There's a dry area back there," he said to Riley. "Help me gather our stuff."

"*Your* stuff. I already have mine right here." He turned, showing Jeff his backpack already on his back under his jacket.

"Fine," Jeff shot back. "Go back where it's dry. I'll get the rest of the stuff."

It didn't take long to grab up the other two backpacks. When he got to the back of the shelter, he threw them down in the dirt.

"I'm cold," Wayne whined. He shivered and leaned against Jeff.

Jeff grabbed Wayne's pack and shoved it at him. "Put on whatever clothes you have in here, then we'll all lay down together to conserve body heat."

Jeff pulled on his extra t-shirt and Levi jacket. It wasn't much, but every little bit helped.

Riley and Wayne pulled on their jackets. All three lay down, shivering on the dirt floor. Jeff had his back to Wayne, who in turn snuggled up against Riley.

Jeff estimated it wasn't really all that cold. The temperature was probably in the mid-seventies. Being wet made it feel colder. *Well, we won't freeze to death, but we are definitely in for a miserable night.*

Just as Jeff's back started to warm up, Wayne said, "I gotta go."

Jeff turned roughly and lost his temper. "Jeez, Wayne, why didn't you go when we were up?"

"'Cause I didn't have to go then."

Irritable, Jeff stood up. The comforting heat immediately disappeared from his back.

Wayne flipped on his little flashlight and moved to the

front of the shelter.

Jeff took a deep breath and unclenched his fists. The last thing he needed to do was blow up again. The surest way to get Wayne crying was to scream and yell at him.

Hearing a noise outside, Jeff looked toward the front of the shelter. *Was that Wayne calling me?* He could see Wayne's little form silently standing outside the entrance next to the rock wall. He looked out into the darkness as he took care of his business. The rain seemed to have stopped falling.

Jeff sat down and leaned against the rock wall. He was so tired he could hardly keep himself awake. *I'll lean my head back for just a minute, just until Wayne's done.*

"Jeff."

This time Jeff was sure he'd heard Wayne's voice, but he was too drowsy to open his eyes. "What?"

"Jeff." The call came louder with a tremor of terror in Wayne's voice.

Rousing himself and fumbling for his flashlight, Jeff bumped into Riley, who had fallen back to sleep.

"Hmmm, what's going on?" Riley mumbled.

"*Jeff!*" Wayne said more insistently.

A chill ran down Jeff's spine. "Get up, Riley. Something's wrong." Jeff scrambled for the flashlight. Turning it on, he franticly searched the ground for the machete, which was nowhere to be seen. He suddenly remembered leaning it against the rock near the entrance.

"*Jeff!*" Wayne now shuffled backward toward the entrance.

In three quick strides, Jeff snatched up the machete. With two more steps, he stood next to Wayne. "What is it?" He added his light to Wayne's small beam, both going out into the blackness.

On the beach, at the edge of the line of trees, two glowing green eyes from some monstrous creature stared at them.

"Get inside. Hurry," Jeff said, pushing Wayne behind him. Walking backward, he stepped into the slushy fire pit and fell flat on his back.

The flashlight flew out of his hand, rolled to a stop against the back wall of the shelter, and shined its light toward the entrance.

Jeff heard something rustling just outside as he scrambled to his feet.

A dark shape burst out of the blackness and slammed into his legs. "*Wraaawoo, wraaawoo, wraaawoo,*" a baby Triceratops bellowed as it ran past him to the back of the shelter.

"Is that the same–?" Wayne started to ask.

"No, it isn't," Riley answered as he focused his flashlight to study the small dinosaur closer. "This one is smaller."

The baby dinosaur whimpered, cowering down against the back wall.

Riley shifted the beam of his flashlight to the dinosaur's face. "Look at his horn, he doesn't have one. Our dino did."

Jeff quickly glanced at the creature. "I wonder why it ran in here," he said, still concerned about the green-eyed animal lurking in the darkness outside. "I wonder if it's the prey of that big dinosaur. That's all we need right now."

An ear-splitting roar made Jeff jump and spin toward the entrance.

Riley lifted his flashlight and illuminated the craggy leering face of a T-Rex just outside, looking in.

"*Jeff!*" Wayne blurted with wide eyes as he tugged on Jeff's jacket.

"Get back," Jeff shouted as they stumbled backward into the corner of the shelter and pressed themselves against the rocks.

The T-Rex stuck its head inside the shelter.

The three of them flattened themselves against the rocks as far back into the V as possible. Shaking with fear, Jeff watched a mouthful of teeth shoot toward them.

Jeff screamed in unison with his brothers.

The T-Rex's head abruptly stopped five feet in front of them. Its hungry eyes glared, but it didn't seem able to move closer. The heavy tree forming the shelter sat too low for the animal to bend down far enough to reach them. With an angry roar, the T-Rex clamped its mouth on a large branch and yanked, attempting to pull the tree off its intended dinner.

Wayne's body trembled. In a high-pitched, shrill voice, he asked, "Can he move the tree?"

"No, he can't," Jeff said with as much confidence as he could muster in his shaky voice. He watched the tree for signs of movement and hoped with all his might that the creature wasn't that strong. "It weighs way too much," he added, seeing that the T-Rex wasn't able to budge the trunk. "I think we're safe for the moment." He swallowed hard. Although the V-shaped rocks and the tree overhead made a good hiding spot, it was also a trap with no way out.

The T-Rex backed up and let out a mighty roar of frustration.

A deep, throaty, *"Wraaawoo, wraaawoo,"* sounded from somewhere in the dark.

The baby dinosaur, huddled in fear against the wall, responded with a low growl followed by two loud grunts.

"I hope that's a call for help," Riley said, clinging tightly to his computer.

"Me, too," Wayne replied. To the baby dinosaur, he said, "I hope your mom and dad come down here and kick that T-Rex's butt."

The baby responded with a whimper, almost as though it had understood Wayne's words.

When Jeff looked up, he realized the baby had whimpered because the T-Rex was coming back inside for a second try.

TAYLOR shot out of his tent, having been awakened by the roar of an animal and the screams of fear coming from the boys. It took him several minutes to reach their shelter. He hid behind a rock to orient himself to what was happening. With his night-vision goggles, he recognized a T-Rex standing at the entrance to the shelter, angrily trying to remove the tree trunk.

Fear for the boys washed over him. He stepped forward preparing himself to shoot the dinosaur before it got to the boys.

As he started to make his way around his hiding place, Taylor was startled to see another dinosaur, one that looked like a huge Triceratops, come running down the beach toward him. The animal let out a loud *Wraaawoo* sound and put in a burst of speed.

With Taylor's new and healthy respect for the speed and size of the dinosaurs, he stepped behind the rock again. He sensed that it wouldn't do well for him to get into the middle of this fight. He only hoped that the boys would survive.

CHAPTER 28

JEFF tried to gather his wits as he watched the T-Rex lay down on its side at the entrance of the shelter and use its tail and one leg to scoot forward.

"Uh, oh," Riley said, pushing up his glasses, "I think we're in trouble now." He pressed further back against the rock, but there was nowhere else to go.

Jeff moved in front of his brothers and held the machete out in front of him. He knew it was crazy, but what else could he do?

The T-Rex covered about two feet with each lunge.

When it reached about ten feet away, Jeff ran forward and slashed it across the face with the machete. It felt like hitting a brick wall with a baseball bat. The force of the impact reverberated up Jeff's arm and almost knocked the machete out of his hand.

The T-Rex roared and shoved itself forward another two feet. Froth and saliva sprayed from its mouth.

"Hit it harder, Jeff," Wayne yelled.

"Yeah," Riley joined in. "Hit it like you're making a mark on a tree."

Jeff ran forward and swung again, aiming for the black oval eye glaring at him. The blade bounced off the outer layer of thick skin without even a cut. He swung again, this time aiming for the end of its nose. The machete did little more damage than before. As Jeff stepped back, he ran into Riley, which told him he was out of room and backed into the shelter as far as he could go.

The T-Rex scooted closer, only four feet away.

Growing angry at having no other options, Jeff lunged forward like a swordsman, pointing the machete at the T-Rex's eye. His aim was off by a few inches, drawing only a little blood on the T-Rex's face.

The T-Rex lunged forward again, closing the remaining distance by two feet.

"*Jeff*," Wayne hollered. "*Do something.*"

Jeff broke out in a cold sweat. Without enough room to maneuver, he saw nothing he could do. One or all of them were going to die in the next few minutes. He spread his arms and backed up against his brothers in a futile attempt to protect them.

The angry T-Rex lunged forward again, its teeth coming within inches of Jeff's stomach. It let out a roar, then started rolling from side to side, slowly moving in the opposite direction.

Jeff stood stiffly in front of his brothers. His eyes widened in disbelief that the creature was going the other way.

"Why's it leaving?" Riley asked as he pushed Jeff's arm away and moved up next to him.

"I don't know," Jeff croaked, his mouth dry as the terror began to dissipate. He heard loud rustling outside and thought he saw a faint movement in the darkness behind the T-Rex.

The T-Rex shot slightly forward again, as if it had been shoved from behind. It roared out of pain, not anger. It moved more quickly to get outside the shelter.

The baby dinosaur moved next to Jeff's legs. It let out a series of grunts, then sat down.

The T-Rex, far enough out in the open, stood up.

Jeff grabbed his flashlight from the dirt. In the powerful beam, he saw two large, gaping slashes flowing with blood on the T-Rex's backside. It roared a challenge to its opponent and charged. It met in an angry clash with a large Triceratops, most likely one of the parents of the baby.

Keeping their flashlights on the dinosaurs, Jeff, Riley, and Wayne watched the fight between two of the most ferocious dinosaurs that ever lived.

The Triceratops managed to get between the T-Rex and the shelter. It proceeded to move the T-Rex down the beach, away from the baby dinosaur.

Jeff walked cautiously with his two brothers to a short, safe distance outside their shelter where they could watch. He pondered that seeing this fight was something no other human had ever witnessed.

The T-Rex's attention stayed on the Triceratops in front of it. It didn't notice the second Triceratops come in from the side. The second Triceratops buried its two long horns into the T-Rex's stomach, then shook its head from side to side. When it stepped back, long strings of the T-Rex's intestines were pulled from its stomach.

"Oh, gross," Wayne said as the T-Rex stepped on its own insides, pulling more out. It fell to its side, thrashing in the sand and screaming its rage to the world.

The baby dinosaur ran outside where it reunited with its parents.

Jeff sighed. What he wouldn't give right now to have someone…anyone…come charging out of the brush and save them from this dangerous world. He knew it was impossible, but he looked around anyway as he grabbed the shoulders of his brothers and they made their way back to the shelter.

"Wow, that was intense," Wayne commented as he slumped against the wall.

Keeping the machete close to him this time, Jeff said, "Let's lie down and try to get a little more sleep while we can."

"Don't you mean *if* we can," Riley said. "After almost being eaten and seeing that bloody fight, I don't think I can go back to sleep."

"If I did," Wayne added, "I'd only have nightmares. I'd rather stay awake."

"Okay," Jeff said, "but let's at least lay together so we can stay warm."

Riley and Wayne both agreed as they cuddled close together.

A short time later, Jeff wasn't surprised that both his brothers had fallen sound asleep. He, on the other hand, couldn't sleep at all. After seeing how easily the T-Rex had been able to get to them, he knew he would be awake, watching the darkness for the rest of the night. He still shivered inside and hoped like hell they would find Mitch and the girls first thing in the morning so they could go home.

As he lay awake, the clouds broke up enough to reveal an almost full moon high in the sky. As he stared at the moonlight glinting off the water of the lake he wondered how Mitch and the girls were doing. Knowing how much Mitch loved camping and how much he knew about wood lore, Jeff was pretty certain they had to be doing better than he and his brothers. Of course, if they had an encounter with a T-Rex or other deadly beast, there was no telling what might have happened to them. He didn't want to think about it.

He turned his attention to the peaceful glow of the moon on the water and thought about his safe life playing video games in Lake Havasu City, Arizona. This spring break had turned out to be far more dramatic than he could have ever imagined.

TAYLOR, having watched the whole affair with the battling dinosaurs, breathed heavily from the aftermath of fear and shock as he made his way back to his tent. He wished he'd been able to bring a camera, but Clemmons had forbidden them to take pictures.

He had stood in awe as the T-Rex backed out of the shelter. The Triceratops slashed at its back before it could get to its feet. It had no chance to take the lead.

Taylor had remained stunned in place as the two large creatures made their way down the beach. He saw the three boys come out of the shelter and watch the battle, too. With a sense of relief that they were okay, he turned back to the battle.

A second Triceratops came in from the side and tossed the T-Rex around on its horn. As the T-Rex crashed to the ground, Taylor pumped his arm in the air at the clever strategy. *Good touch.*

After the night grew quiet, Taylor waited until the boys went back into the shelter and turned off their flashlights.

Still almost breathless from the larger-than-life battle of beasts, Taylor stepped into his tent and pulled out his book. He knew he wouldn't be able to get back to sleep. Using a small light, he read the pages, ate a candy bar, and listened vigilantly for any unusual sounds as he impatiently waited for dawn.

CHAPTER 29

TERRY felt something tickling his nose. He reached his hand up to scratch the itch and felt something scurry across his cheek. His eyes flew open and he sat up, wincing at the pain in his ribs and slamming the top of his head just above his hair line into something hard. It almost knocked him out.

"What's going on?" he mumbled as he shook his head and tried to focus his eyes. Everything was dark. It took him a moment to remember he had bedded down, wrapped with cotton-covered branches, in a jumble of rocks in the middle of a jungle.

He started feeling lots of things crawling all over his body. Suddenly, it dawned on him. Maybe that wasn't *cotton* he'd seen last night. Maybe it was some kind of web or cocoon. With his inclination to imagine things, he wasn't sure if the tickling feelings were real or if they had come from his mind playing tricks on him.

Repulsed at the thought of bugs of any kind, real or imagined, crawling over him, he panicked. He threw off the branches and winced in pain at his broken arm and broken rib, which he'd forgotten in his hurry. Groaning, he held his broken arm close to his side and shifted slightly toward the entrance of his shelter. He could see a dim light, moonlight, coming in from the outside. He smelled rain. Close to the opening, he started to crawl outside when a huge head swung toward him. He quickly ducked back inside just as the head pushed up against the opening, blocking off all light.

Squirming at the sensation of tickling little creatures, Terry was torn between not getting eaten and the need to get the creepy-crawlers off his body. He felt his anger rising.

Losing his temper, he balled up the fist of his good hand and punched the dinosaur as hard as he could. One, two, three times. It felt like hitting a bag full of sand.

"Damn," Terry yelled in frustration as he swung again. His hand slid into a warm moist opening that he thought might be the dinosaur's nostrils. Warm air flowed across his arm. Thinking the inside of the dinosaur's nose would be sensitive, he opened his fist and jammed his fingers into the soft flesh. When nothing happened, he grabbed for the tendrils that stuck up like hair and pulled as hard as he could.

With a loud grunt the head pulled away.

Scooting to the edge of the shelter, Terry saw the dinosaur walking away. *Well, at least he's not interested in eating me.* He squeezed through the opening.

Out in the open, the light of the full moon allowed Terry to see what had been crawling over his body for the last five minutes. Spiders. *Large* spiders.

Dancing around, he used his good arm to rip the buttons off his shirt as he tore the shirt open. He shook the shirt free of spiders and used it to brush his head, chest, and back. He quickly stripped off the rest of his clothes and used the shirt to make sure he was spider-free.

Sensing something still tickling his forehead, he wiped it with his shirt, but instead of finding a spider, he found blood. *Must have split my head open when I cracked it on that rock.*

He gathered up his clothes and shook them out carefully. When he was certain everything was spider-free, he looked for spider bites, but didn't find any. He started dressing again, using his good arm. He'd ripped off all but two buttons in his haste to remove the shirt, so he left it open.

To make matters worse, he hadn't been imagining things when he thought he'd smelled rain. It had rained sometime during the night and the ground was wet and muddy. His pants and underwear were now wet and muddy, too. He shivered as he pulled them on.

Better to be a little cold than run around buck-naked. He smiled at the thought, imagining himself completely naked, running through the brush and being chased by a dinosaur. *Don't want that.*

After dressing, he looked at his watch and was surprised to see that he'd slept longer than he'd thought. *It's after four. Good. Only a few more hours until the sun comes up.*

A thought flashed through his mind. *Then what?* He wasn't sure he wanted to think about the answer to that question. He would rather deal with that dark subject in the bright light of day.

Knowing he probably wouldn't sleep again, he decided to make his way back to the creek and wait until the sun came up. The moon gave him enough light to see as long as he stayed out of the shadows.

It didn't take long before he heard the comfortable sound of water gurgling across rocks. It had taken him maybe a half-hour to reach the creek. After a soothing drink, he sat on a large rock and waited for the sun to come up. Not until then would he face the questions trying to force their way into his thoughts, the worst one being, *Did Riley go home? Am I the only human in this world?*

JUST before dawn, when Osborne awoke and got up to check on Terry, he wasn't surprised to see Terry gone from the shelter. He observed the remains of the cottony branches strewn across the shelter haphazardly. He shook his head.

Osborne had seen the same kind of cottony branches in the past and knew full well that they weren't cotton, but spider webs. Although he felt bad he hadn't warned Terry, his orders were orders. He wasn't about to reveal himself just to save Terry a little discomfort. Osborne shrugged. The spiders were harmless to humans, but he knew they could give a person nightmares if that person had a phobia about spiders. From what Osborne knew about Terry and had observed, Terry seemed to have a lot of hang-ups.

Already packed and ready to go, Osborne followed Terry's muddy tracks until he came near the creek. Not wanting Terry to see him, he climbed a tree and ate his breakfast while he waited for it to get lighter.

CHAPTER 30

A sharp sting on Jeff's left hand brought him out of a deep sleep. He slapped at his hand to kill whatever creature had stung him. He opened his eyes.

"*Crap,*" he yelped when he saw a trail of one-inch-long black ants marching toward him in the morning light. The enormous pincers on the ants looked like something that could take a big chunk of meat out of someone's skin.

He jumped to his feet and moved out of their path. He checked his hand and arm for more ants. Luckily, he found none. The sting had come from a single scout, roaming ahead of the pack and looking for food. He now had a big red welt on his hand.

Shuddering, Jeff turned to check on Riley and Wayne, sound asleep and curled up together in a ball. Seeing that they were free of crawling insects, he decided to let them sleep a little longer. He kept an eye on the ants to make sure they didn't divert their path toward his brothers. Thinking they were safe, he moved off a little ways from the shelter and relieved his bladder.

He welcomed the early morning sun after such a long, miserable night. The temperature had dropped in the shelter during the last part of the darkened hours. He tilted back his head for a moment, closed his eyes, and relished the warmth of the life-giving light just breaking over the eastern hills.

Relieved that they'd survived through the horrific night, he had a good feeling about the coming day.

Inside the shelter, he nudged Riley with the toe of his hiking shoe. "Come on, sleepy heads, time to get up. We'll eat breakfast, then we'll go find Carlita, Mitch, and Macy."

He kept his voice light and positive, hoping to give his brothers a sense of courage and safety.

TERRY shifted restlessly on a large rock next to the bubbling creek. Sounds of early morning insects filled the air as the sun came over the mountain, but other than that, all was quiet as questions ran amuck in his mind. *Did Riley and his group go home? Am I the only human in the world? How will I survive? How will I make fire or get food? How can I make a shelter? How long can I survive without these things? Do I even want to try?*

Despite the bravado in his thoughts at times, he knew he wouldn't last longer than a week, at most, probably more likely three or four days. That's how long he figured it would take a hungry dinosaur to find and eat him. He held no illusions that he could evade all the ravenous predators stalking through the brush and looking for an easy meal. He would be easy to catch. He couldn't run as fast as any of the dinosaurs he'd seen so far. And worse, as he grew weak from lack of food, he would slow down even more.

The sun chased away the darkness, allowing Terry to clearly see his surroundings. Nothing could chase the dark thoughts out of his mind as a feeling of depression began to overwhelm him.

Don't dwell on the negative, he told himself, but it was hard to get beyond the fears in his mind. He couldn't imagine what he would do if Riley and his group didn't show up in the next few hours.

His stomach growled angrily at not having eaten for over twenty-four hours. Distracting himself from his morbid thoughts, he decided to explore the surrounding area to look for berries or fruit. He groaned in pain as he stood up. His broken rib and arm had stiffened up while he'd sat hunched against the cool air of the early morning.

He hiked to the far west side of the clearing and stood in the direct sunshine. It's warmth seeped deeply into his body and felt good. He closed his eyes and took in the warmth, starting to feel better about his situation. True he didn't have any tools or weapons, but he could make some out of rocks. He could find an outcropping of obsidian to make knifes and spear points. If he couldn't find obsidian, he knew flint, jasper, or chert would work almost as well. With his eyes closed, he imagined everything he would need to do.

With flint, he could make a fire with his nail clippers, which were made of steel. With a fire, a spear, and a knife, he would have a fifty/fifty chance of surviving the first month. If he made it that long, his odds of surviving the first year would jump to about seventy-five percent.

A big question passed through his mind: Did he want to survive? What kind of life would it be if he were the only human in the world? How long would it take before he started talking to himself just to hear a friendly voice?

He chuckled to himself at the irony. He'd always wanted to be alone, to be isolated from everyone in the world. And now, maybe he got his wish.

He supposed he could capture an animal and try to make a pet out of it. He knew small mammals existed in this era, animals that he hadn't seen yet. Nothing as large as a horse or cow, but possibly something like a large dog. *A dog would be nice. I could train it to help me hunt. It could also help protect me by warning me if a large dinosaur was sneaking up on us.*

His stomach growled almost as loudly as a dinosaur's roar in the jungle. If he didn't find something to eat soon, he'd end up getting weak.

He walked into the thick jungle-like vegetation and kept an eye out for fruits, nuts, and berries. It didn't take long to discover wild berries growing all over the place. Taking a huge leaf off a tree, he used it as a basket to pile up a stack of berries.

Returning to the creek, he sat on the bank and ate his breakfast. He washed it down with cool, sweet water. When he was done, he lay on his back in the sun and dozed contentedly.

WITH Riley and Wayne packed up and waiting for him on the trail, Jeff stood at the entrance of the shelter and took one last look to make sure they hadn't left anything behind. In the light of day, his eyes swept across the area quickly. He would miss this little nook where he went one-on-one with one of the most ferocious animals that had ever lived. Feeling different about himself somehow, he shrugged and hurried to catch up with his brothers.

"It's a shame to see such a magnificent animal dead," Riley said as they passed the gory body of the T-Rex, now swarmed with ugly-looking vulture-like birds.

"Better him than us," Jeff said. He picked up the pace, following the tracks they'd made the night before, now muddy holes from the rain. Coming to the opening in the brush, he made his brothers stop as he carefully checked to see that no dinosaurs were using the trail. He would have followed the shoreline back to the stream, but a large outcropping of rock that extended out into the water blocked that option.

For some unknown reason, Jeff felt confident and sure of himself today. He looked at the machete in his hand. Maybe his new feelings arose out of the fact he'd faced down a T-Rex with nothing but this machete. Or maybe it was just the morning sunshine making him feel hopeful. Whatever the reason, he bounced along in a good mood and had high hopes the day would turn out to be in their favor.

SEVERAL hours later, Jeff recognized the area near the small brook where they'd been separated from Mitch and the girls the day before.

Feeling disappointed at not seeing them, Jeff slumped to the ground. "Damn, I was hoping they'd be here."

"Maybe they're on their way," Wayne said hopefully as he bent down to get a drink.

Riley sat on a rock. "Let's give them a little while. I'm sure they'll show up." He held his computer protectively on his lap. He seemed sullen and withdrawn.

Jeff couldn't help but wonder if Riley and Wayne really believed what they were saying, or if they were just trying to put on a brave front like he was. In truth, he grew more concerned now. He'd really believed Mitch and the girls would be waiting for them here.

Suddenly, another thought struck him. *I wonder if they're at the meadow where we first arrived. Back where Mitch had left his gun case. Is it possible Mitch thought we would go there instead of here?* Not sure what Mitch would have done, Jeff decided to wait for a while and see if they showed up.

Wayne finished drinking and wandered next to Jeff. "Why don't we build a signal fire that puts out lots of smoke. That way, if Mitch is anywhere close, he'll know we're here."

Wishing he'd been as bright to think of that, Jeff stood up and said, "Good idea. Why don't the two of you gather wood while I get the fire going?"

Ten minutes later, he had a fire roaring in an open clearing from the dry kindling collected from under the trees and bushes. He chopped branches off a pine tree and laid them across the fire. The lack of wind allowed the thick, dark smoke to billow straight up into the pristine blue sky. If Mitch was within twenty miles, he'd be able to see it. Jeff hoped that was the case, since he didn't want to think about the idea that Mitch and the girls had already met their fate from hungry dinosaurs.

CHAPTER 31

MITCH woke to the sound of a blood-curdling scream. He bolted upright, temporarily confused. He blinked and rubbed his eyes, trying to get them to work in the bright, morning sunshine.

Carlita and Macy both yelled, "Mitch, help."

Remembering where he was, his eyes locked on the tent, then narrowed in anger. Ten or so of the little hyena-looking dinos circled and sniffed the base of the tent. Two tugged and tore at opposite corners, trying to bite their way in. He must have been sleeping pretty heavily for them to get so close.

Lifting his rifle, he fired a shot into the air, earning him another scream from the girls.

Some of the dinos jumped and looked around in surprise, but none of them moved from the tent. Putting the rifle to his shoulder, he centered the crosshairs of the scope on the head of the largest dino, which stood on the far periphery of the group like a general watching over his troops.

Because the dino was so close, Mitch's view through the scope was blurred, but still, he hit right where he'd hoped. The big bullet flipped the dino head over heels. It landed ten feet farther away from the tent than it had been.

After a few seconds the smell of blood drew the attention of the other dinos. Leaving the tent in favor of a more readily accessible meal, the dinos tore into their hapless companion.

While they were busy, Mitch unzipped the tent door. "Hurry, grab the blankets and get out of here."

Carlita, half-carrying Macy, wasted no time getting to the relative safety of the other side of the fire pit.

Grabbing the tent by its top, Mitch dragged it after him as

he followed the girls. Dropping the tent on the far side of the fire pit, he knelt down and hurriedly stirred the ashes until he found hot coals. Even though it had rained lightly during the night, it hadn't completely put out their fire.

Laying small sticks on top of the coals, Mitch gently blew until the flames sprang up and tickled the kindling. He continued laying down bigger and bigger sticks until the fire blazed three feet high. Feeling safe near the roaring fire, he turned to see how the girls were doing. Other than their mussed hair and their eyes wide with fear, they both looked fine.

JEFF jumped to his feet as a gunshot echoed across the hills. Another followed closely. "Did you hear that?" he cried out in joy. "It has to be Mitch."

Riley and Wayne both stood on their feet as well. Excitement glittered in Wayne's eyes, but Riley's showed fear. Fear of what, Jeff couldn't tell. Maybe Riley was frightened Mitch and the girls were in trouble. Maybe he worried Mitch would lead another T-Rex back to them. Maybe he was just scared of everything. Jeff couldn't blame him. He was a little scared himself.

"Should we go look for him?" Wayne asked.

"No," Jeff replied. "I'm sure he's headed this way. We'll stay here and keep the fire burning, just in case he needs it to help him find his way."

"Hey, maybe he smelled the smoke and fired his gun to let us know he's on his way," Wayne said eagerly. Turning he called over his shoulder, "I'll climb a tree and see if I can see them."

Not wanting to dash Wayne's hopes, Jeff let him go. Turning to Riley, he said, "You okay? You seem…I don't know…you're not acting like your usual self."

He adjusted his glasses. "I'm fine. I'm just ready to go home. I never should have gone the first time, let alone brought all of you here." His eyes darted around nervously and one hand busily twisted the tail of his shirt. "I need a drink," he said as he turned and walked away, his computer clutched tightly under one arm.

Jeff stared after him. Something wasn't right, but if Riley didn't want to talk about it, he wasn't going to force him.

As soon as Mitch caught up with them, they'd be back home. Everything would go back to normal. Moving to the fire, he piled more green branches on top of it to increase the smoke. *Come on, Mitch. We're ready to go home.*

THE distant boom of a gunshot startled Terry out of a sound sleep. He froze for a few seconds. His body might have been immobile, but his mind stayed busy, rejoicing in the fact he hadn't been deserted. Now, he just had to figure out from which direction the gunshot had come.

High on hope, his eyes scanned the sky above the tree tops as if he could glean a clue from the heavens. As he faced westward, another shot broke the silence. *No doubt about it, that came from over there.*

Terry's body automatically turned a few degrees to the left, stopping in a southwesterly direction. Refusing to lose contact with Riley's group again, he took off running through an open area. As the brush thickened, he desperately searched for trails to take him in the general direction he wanted to go. When one trail started veering off, he found another.

"LET me get this tent put away, then I'll fix breakfast," Mitch said as he checked to make sure the hyenas were still busy with their own breakfast and not sneaking up on them.

As it turned out, he hadn't needed the fire after all. Even thought the dinos were only twenty feet away, they weren't paying attention to the three of them.

"I don't want breakfast," Carlita demanded harshly. "I want to go home."

Sighing, Mitch said, "I promise we'll go home, but we need to find Jeff, Riley, and Wayne first. I don't know about you, but I need some nourishment if I'm gonna be hiking around all day." He looked at his watch to see it was after 9:30. Surprised, he knew they must have been really tired last night to sleep in so late.

"I think we should eat, too," Macy said, keeping her eye on the dinos as she edged as close to the fire as possible. "But let's make it quick, okay?"

Moving to his pack, Mitch dug inside one oversized pocket. "This quick enough for you?" he asked as he threw each of them a breakfast bar.

"You'd better have that tent packed and ready to go by the time I'm done eating," Carlita demanded as she tore open her package. "Because we're leaving as soon as this is gone."

Mitch was already taking the tent apart. Within two minutes, he had it stowed in his pack. Carlita relented and gave him an extra five minutes to make sure the fire was safely out. Throwing his pack on his back, he picked up his rifle and was ready to go.

"What about my ankle?" Macy asked.

Mitch handed her the crutch he'd made. "I hope it's the right height."

A smile lit her face. Mitch had rolled up one of his shirts and covered the fork of the Y, providing some padding so Macy wouldn't rub her armpit raw. "It fits perfectly," she said as she followed Carlita out of camp.

Munching on his own breakfast bar and feeling good about himself, he sauntered along behind Carlita and Macy.

CHAPTER 32

TERRY had covered about a mile when the trails stopped going southwesterly. For some reason, he couldn't explain why every trail seemed to head east/west. He stood at the juncture of two small trails that came together to form one large trail heading due east.

He had two choices: make his own trail through the brush or follow the large trail to the east. He wondered if the large trail would eventually take him back to the creek. *That might not be such a bad idea.* He licked his dry lips. *From the creek, I might be able to find another trail heading southwest.*

Terry had no idea how far the gunshot had traveled, but he felt sure he hadn't gone far enough yet. *Maybe I'm close enough that if I yell, they'll hear me.* At this point, he didn't care if he was exposed. It was his only hope of not being left behind.

He cupped his hands around his mouth, took a deep breath, and smelled smoke. Dropping his hands, he took another breath to make sure he wasn't imagining things.

That's definitely smoke. I must be fairly close to their camp.

Now, he wasn't sure if he should yell or not. If he remained hidden from them, he could steal Riley's computer and keep to his original plan. The idea of being the only person in the world with a time machine bolstered his self-worth and courage. *Maybe things are going to turn out okay after all.*

With a new bounce in his step, he started down the trail, following his nose to what he imagined would be a joyous occasion for him. *And a shocking one for Riley.*

He grinned maliciously.

"DO you see that?" Carlita asked Mitch from her position in the lead as she came up over a hill.

Joining her, Mitch saw a column of smoke rising to the sky. From this location, the brush and trees had thinned just enough to allow him to see further than twenty feet in any direction.

Macy looked nervously at all the brush surrounding them. "Is it a forest fire?"

"Nope," Mitch replied confidently, seeing that the fire seemed to be contained. "It's Jeff and the boys." He shook his head in wonder as they continued to walk toward the smoke. "I don't know if Jeff thought of it or one of his brothers, but building a signal fire was a great idea."

"It sure was," Carlita agreed. "Now we can go home." She momentarily quickened her pace, but soon turned back to check on Macy, who couldn't keep up on her crutch.

"How far away do you think they are?" Macy asked.

Mitch studied the smoke and the terrain. "Maybe a half-mile, a mile at the most. We could be there in an hour, depending on how fast you can travel, Macy."

Macy stopped and grimaced. Shyly, she said, "We would get there faster if you carried me. Are you up to it?"

"Hell, yeah," he blurted, his energy renewed with the idea that they would soon be home. He bent down.

Holding her crutch in one hand, Macy leaned across his right shoulder, her upper body resting on his backpack.

"Double-time it, Carlita," he bellowed as he stood up and adjusted Macy's weight. "I'm ready to go home, too."

JEFF paced restlessly back and forth in front of the fire.

He only hoped the gunshots had meant that Mitch and the girls were in the vicinity and not battling some kind of ferocious animals.

"What's taking them so long?" Wayne whined for the third time. He'd gotten tired of looking from up in the tree after only five minutes when he'd realized he couldn't see Mitch and the girls in the thick brush.

"They could have been a long ways away," Jeff replied in as positive a voice as he could muster. He cut another branch off a pine tree for the fire. "It might take them hours to get here." It had been a little over an hour since they'd heard the gunshot, and like Wayne, Jeff had been hoping to see Mitch and the girls come strolling into the little clearing at any time. Knowing they were so close to being able to go home, he started to get more anxious, especially watching Riley, who had been avoiding him and Wayne all morning.

Riley suddenly stood up. "Shhh, I hear something." He stared at the west side of the clearing where a large trail had been made through the brush.

From where Jeff stood, he couldn't see very far down the trail, but he didn't want to step out and expose himself from behind the safety of the pine tree if a T-Rex or some other nasty dinosaur suddenly appeared.

JEFF'S heart about burst out of his chest when he saw Carlita come into sight. "Man, am I glad to see you," Jeff called out as he rushed to take her into his arms. "I was so worried about you," he whispered into her ear.

"Are you and the boys okay?" she asked, pulling back slightly and looking toward Riley and Wayne.

"Physically we're fine." He lowered his voice. "Something's wrong with Riley. He seems…" His voice trailed off when he saw Mitch coming up the trail with Macy on his back. "Macy, are you okay?"

Huffing and puffing, Mitch carefully set Macy down next to the fire.

She used her crutch to steady herself. "I'm fine. I twisted my ankle yesterday." She looked at Wayne, who now stood next to Jeff, then at Riley, who sat down on his rock. "Are you guys okay?" she asked with arched brows.

"Yeah, dude, is everything good?" Mitch's eyes flicked to Riley as he slipped off his pack and leaned his rifle against it.

Jeff shrugged. "We're not hurt or anything." He lowered his voice again. "I'm not sure what's wrong with him." He tipped his head in Riley's direction.

"I'll have a talk with him in a minute," Mitch said as he headed for the brook to get a drink.

"I'll talk to him," Carlita offered, but Jeff grabbed her arm, stopping her.

"Let Mitch do it. You know, they have a special relationship. If anyone can get Riley to open up, it's Mitch."

She studied Riley, as though analyzing his mood. "You're right," she said. "He's in one of his just-leave-me-alone moods. He'd never open up to me."

Jeff sensed she wanted to go to Riley and comfort him, so he put his arm around her shoulder and hugged her.

Mitch got his drink from the brook and talked quietly to Riley.

Wayne and Jeff told their experiences of the night to Carlita and Macy as the four of them started putting out the fire with water and dirt.

While Wayne extolled Jeff's bravery in the face of the hungry T-Rex, Jeff kept an eye on Riley, wondering what was going on. He grew increasingly anxious to get going out of this dangerous world before another T-Rex showed up.

CHAPTER 33

JEFF threw dirt on the last of the fire as he watched Mitch rejoin their circle, followed by a reluctant, devastated-looking Riley. Mitch's face seemed pinched.

"What's going on?" Macy asked.

"We've got a little problem," Mitch said, staring at Riley, who kept his head down and his computer clutched tightly to his chest.

Carlita stepped forward and demanded, "Well, what is it? We want to get going."

Mitch nudged Riley, who finally looked up.

Riley slowly looked each of them in the eye before he blurted, "I lost the extra battery to my computer."

Sensing something more, Jeff's anger began to rise. "Please tell me the battery you have in the computer isn't dead." He held his breath, dreading Riley's answer.

"Not completely."

"Does it have enough power to get us home?" Macy said in a pleading tone.

"I think so." He bowed his head again, acting as though he were ashamed.

"What's going on, Riley?" Carlita asked gently.

"It's my fault," Riley whispered, almost on the verge of tears.

Carlita knelt down to Riley's eyelevel.

Jeff clenched his fists, wanting to scream at Riley for the stupidity of his carelessness.

Mitch put a finger to his lips, motioning everybody to be quiet and not interrupt.

"Last night," Riley said softly, "I woke up and couldn't

sleep, so I turned my computer on and played a game."

"And?" she prodded.

"I fell asleep and left my computer on, which almost completely drained the battery."

"And what happened to your spare battery?"

Riley held up his backpack. "It was in here." He showed her one of the side pockets with a tear across the bottom. "It must have slipped out sometime yesterday. I didn't notice it was gone until I went to replace the dead battery this morning." His voice cracked and his lip trembled, but he didn't cry. "I'm sorry."

Jeff's mind whirled with dread. He couldn't even speak at the thought of what would happen if Riley's computer didn't get them home.

Mitch put an arm on Riley's shoulder. "Hey, I'm sure it's got enough juice for one jump through time left in it. After all, all you have to do is turn it on and punch the button, right, dude?" He smiled down at Riley.

A tear formed in Riley's eye. "Yeah, something like that."

Wayne inched his way next to Jeff. "Um...Riley?" He held his hand out, palm up. "I saw the battery fall out and I picked it–"

"*You little twerp,*" Riley yelled as he snatched the battery out of Wayne's hand. "Why didn't you tell me you had it all this time?"

Now, Wayne's bottom lip quivered, tears formed in his eyes, and his chin dropped to his chest. "With everything that happened yesterday, I forgot."

Jeff wanted to shake both of his brothers for putting them through this torment.

"Hey, don't be too hard on the little guy," Mitch said as he put an arm around Wayne's shoulders. "We ought to be thanking him for picking it up. If not, we might've been here for a long, long time."

"That's right." Carlita pulled Wayne into a bear hug. Squeezing him, she smiled at Riley.

"Okay, okay," Riley said. "I'm sorry for yelling at you, Wayne, but I've been worried sick that we wouldn't be able to get home and..."

Jeff heard a faint whisper that quickly rose to a loud roar.

"Get down," Mitch yelled as he tackled Macy to the ground.

Jeff hit the dirt, unsure of what was happening.

The roar passed overhead.

Jeff looked up to see a bird the size of a small plane swoop past their prone figures.

Squawking, the bird pumped its wings and lifted itself over the trees, quickly disappearing from sight.

"Is everybody okay?" Jeff asked from the ground.

Nods and muttered yeses came back in confirmation.

"I'm so sick of this place," he said as he stood up and brushed the dirt and grass from his pants. "Riley, get your computer ready. As soon as we hit the clearing where we arrived, we're going home."

"You got that right, dude," Mitch said enthusiastically as he pulled his pack on and picked up his rifle. "Macy, can you walk for awhile? I'm not sure I can carry you much more."

Before she answered, Jeff stepped forward. "I'll carry her for a little bit if it will help us get home sooner."

Mitch laughed. "This I gotta see."

Jeff made a face. "What? You don't think I can carry her?" He bent down to let Macy lie across his shoulder in the way that Mitch had carried her.

"Oh, I think you can carry her," Mitch said, "but how far you can carry her is another story." He led off without another word.

Carlita smiled as she walked past Jeff. "Even if you can only carry her a little ways, it will help."

Jeff grunted as he stood up with his new load. "You two go ahead." He nodded to Riley and Wayne. "I'll bring up the rear."

As Jeff trudged along behind them, he thought about how he had surprised even himself with his offer to carry Macy. Feeling stronger and more confident about himself, he determined to be of more help in getting everyone safely home.

TERRY stood next to a smoldering fire pit ten minutes later. Someone had damped it with dirt and water, but the fire hadn't gone completely out. For just a moment, he debated whether or not to revive it. If Riley had already used his computer to take his group home, this would be the easiest fire Terry would ever possess.

Frustrated at having missed them, he looked around. They couldn't have been gone very long. Organizing his thoughts, Terry knew Riley hadn't been able to control the location where he'd gone, only the time period. So, he was betting Riley and his companions wouldn't want to pop back into their timeline and appear standing in the middle of a road or something even worse, like in the center of a store, someone else's house, or a public place. That meant they were probably en-route to the clearing where they'd arrived the day before. He needed to hurry and catch them. Their most logical route would be the same one they'd used the day before, the one that followed the creek.

Sure enough, fresh footprints appeared along the bank. Not wanting to take any chances on missing them again, he moved as fast as he could, ignoring his aching arm and rib. He broke into a jog in the open level places.

He sweat as he ran. *I only hope I don't run into any dinosaurs and have to detour out of my way.*

He passed the clump of brush where he'd picked the spider-covered branches, an indication he was getting closer to the clearing. Feeling more and more panicky about them leaving him behind, he kept up his pace, not caring this time if he came upon them abruptly. It might scare them, but at least they wouldn't leave without him. He was tired of this place and wanted to go home.

JEFF gave it his all, but he could only carry Macy for about a quarter-mile. Setting her down, he fell on his back and gasped for air.

Mitch's smiling face peered down at him. "You actually made it farther than I thought you would, dude. I'm impressed. I guess you're in better shape than I thought."

"I didn't want you to have all the fun," Jeff replied as he sat up and took a sip of water from his canteen. His hands shook so badly, he had a hard time keeping the canteen lined up with his mouth. Water dribbled down his chin. It wasn't until he lowered the canteen that he realized it wasn't him shaking. It was the ground.

"Um, guys. What's happening now?" Macy asked, her green eyes wide and glancing fearfully around.

"Is it another stampede?" Carlita asked.

It sounded like a freight train coming through the jungle. The low rumble, at first far away, grew in intensity.

Mitch spread his legs, trying to keep his balance as the earth shimmied and swayed beneath them. "It's an earthquake," he yelled over the roar. "Everybody grab hold of a tree and hold on."

Yeah, right. Jeff couldn't get to a tree, let alone hold on to one.

Suddenly with a ear-shattering roar, the ground ten feet from Jeff split open.

Macy screamed as she teetered on the edge. Arms flailing and red hair flying, she plunged into the abyss.

PICKING his way through a stretch of rocks, Terry heard the kids just ahead of him. As he quickly moved closer to their position, he suddenly couldn't stay on his feet. The ground bucked and swayed, dislodging rocks, which bounced dangerously around his hiking boots. A rock the size of a bowling ball struck his calf, knocking his leg out from underneath him. He fell on his uninjured right side, crashing to the ground. He slammed his head on a rock. The earth still moved, throwing him around, bouncing him off rocks and trees. Writhing in agony, he had to ride it out. He knew earthquakes didn't normally last very long, just a minute or two.

The earth being torn apart sounded so loud, Terry almost didn't hear the scream. *It's one of the girls. They are still here.* If they left without him, he would rather die than be alone forever.

Desperate to get to them, he tried to get up, but the earth rolled him one way, then another. Blood from his new head wound splattered across the rocks and dirt. He tried to protect his arm and rib, but he had no control over his body or movements. It seemed worse than one of his freezing spells.

Resigned to his fate, he only hoped a tree wouldn't fall on him...but then again, maybe it would be for the best. In his current shape, it would be hard to move quickly enough to get to the clearing. He wasn't sure if he would be able to find Riley and his group before they used the time machine to go home. If it were him, he'd use it immediately and take his chances about where he would come back into his own world. *Hell, I'm surprised they haven't already left.*

Bouncing off a large rock, he hit his head again. This time it was too much. He let the blessed blackness take him away.

CHAPTER 34

JEFF desperately tried to get a grip on the branches of a nearby bush as Mitch yelled for Macy after she'd fallen over the edge of the abyss. Trying to crawl across the bucking ground, Mitch was thrown around like a rag doll being bounced on a trampoline.

Frightened by the prospects of what could happen to all of them, Jeff felt helpless, knowing there was nothing he could do but ride it out. He just hoped the opening Macy had fallen into wouldn't close up and bury her. His brothers seemed to be holding their own a safe distance from the crack.

Carlita screamed as a huge redwood came crashing down some twenty feet from her position. The tree fell across the opening where Macy had disappeared, creating a bridge that spanned both sides.

Spread-eagle on the ground, Jeff prayed the earth would stop shaking and that no more trees would fall and crush them.

Finally, the ground stopped moving. An ominous silence briefly filled the air.

Mitch jumped to his feet and ran toward the crack. "Macy, can you hear me? Are you okay?"

Scrambling after Mitch, Jeff slid to a stop at the edge of the fresh gap in front of him, surprised to see how big it was. The quake had split the earth in two, forming a crevasse thirty feet across and ten feet higher on the other side. It stretched farther than he could see in the other directions. The bottom seemed to have no limit.

Mitch, Riley, Wayne, and Carlita all stood next to Jeff, peering down into the opening for a sign of Macy.

"Can anybody see her?" Carlita asked. She leaned over so far she started to fall.

Mitch grabbed her arm. "We don't need you to fall in, too," he said as he pulled her to safety.

Jeff's mouth went dry, fearing that Macy was out of their reach. In a desperate attempt to see her, he climbed out onto the fallen tree. "I see her," he cried out elatedly. "She's lying on a narrow shelf about thirty feet down. Macy can you hear me? Are you okay?"

He got no response.

"How deep is this thing?" Mitch asked.

Jeff looked down below him for the first time. His stomach flip-flopped as a wave of dizziness washed over him.

The gash in the earth appeared to be over a hundred feet deep. It had split the path of the stream, now emptying into the huge hole, slowly eating away at the exposed bank as it followed the new course. Along both sides of the gap, rocks constantly fell out of the soft dirt.

Macy whimpered on the ledge. She moved slightly.

She's alive. Jeff's heart skipped a beat as he noticed that the shelf on which she lay was slowly collapsing. He had to do something before it was too late. "Hang on, Macy," he shouted. "We'll get you out of there in just a minute."

Mitch's face was full of fear as he called out to Jeff, "So, what's the deal?"

Jeff carefully made his way off the tree. Even though Mitch had a lot more knowledge about survival and outdoor emergencies, Jeff knew that this situation called for teamwork, and he would have to take an important role if Macy was to be rescued before the ledge collapsed. "Do you have a rope in your pack?"

"Yeah." Mitch quickly shed his pack. Digging into one of the outside pockets, he came up with a coil of nylon rope.

Jeff took it and headed for a tall tree rooted a safe distance from the edge. He threw off his pack. "Tie off and lower me down, fast." The idea of going down to get her scared the hell out of him, but he knew he wouldn't be able to handle Mitch's weight in bringing them both back up.

Mitch was about to argue about being the one to go down,

when Jeff barked, "I'm lighter, Mitch. I need your strength up here to pull us up."

Carlita grabbed his arm. "What's going on? Is Macy okay?"

He yanked free, knowing every second they delayed put Macy that much closer to plunging into the depths of the earth. "The ledge isn't stable. It's going to collapse." He took one end of the rope and made a slip-loop about eight inches across as he'd learned in summer camp. He made another, bigger one, about ten feet up the rope and put it around his chest, just under his arms. Running to the edge of the hole he tightened the loop around his chest. "Mitch, you ready?"

"Ready, bro."

Jeff stopped at the edge of the crevasse and turned around.

Mitch had the rope going around the tree and then around his waist. He would let the rope out slowly, using the tree trunk friction to stop the ropes progress if he needed to.

Jeff took a deep breath and stepped over the side. Leaning back, he was glad he'd learned to rappel two summers before. As the rope lowered him, he watched where he put his feet. He didn't want to knock a big rock loose and have it fall on Macy…or worse, collapse the ledge.

"Stop," he yelled to Mitch when he was about two feet above the shelf. He came to a stop above Macy's prone form. "Macy, can you hear me?"

"Yes," she whispered, her voice quivering in fear.

"It's gonna be okay. I'm not gonna let you fall." He leaned out and reached his right hand down until it touched her right hand.

She jerked at the unexpected contact and the shelf started to go.

Jeff quickly slipped the eight-inch loop around her wrist and yanked.

The shelf fell away with a loud rumble, nearly drowning out Macy's scream as she plummeted downward.

Jeff thought his ribs were going to break when Macy hit the end of the rope attached to her arm.

She screamed louder as her shoulder almost yanked out of the socket.

He realized now he should have shortened the ten feet of rope between himself and Macy's wrist, but he'd wanted to make sure he had extra length in case he needed it. From above, rocks, loose dirt, and yells of concern pelted him. He ignored it all and concentrated on his situation. "Macy, are you okay?"

"No, my shoulder hurts. I can't stay like this." She moaned in pain.

"I'm going to help you in just a minute. Can you find somewhere to plant your feet so you can take the weight off your arm?" The rope around his chest burned, like he was being cut in two as she flailed around, trying to get a foothold.

Suddenly, the weight hanging off him was gone. Fearfully, he looked down, half-expecting her to be gone.

She perched spread-eagle on the cliff with the left side of her face buried in the dirt.

Jeff yelled, "Mitch, I've got her. But I need you to lower me down about ten feet…slowly."

A cheer came from above.

Jeff felt himself going down. Mitch timed it perfectly and Jeff came to a stop right next to Macy. Swinging his body so it was directly over hers, he said, "I need you to let go with your right hand, okay?"

"No, I can't. I'll fall."

"You won't fall. I've got you, I promise."

She took a deep ragged breath and slowly let it out. She carefully let go.

Jeff widened the knot around her wrist and moved the rope up until it was under her right shoulder. "Okay, now you can put that hand back and tilt your head back just far enough for me to get the rope over it." He didn't have to tell her to let go with her left hand, she did it herself.

As soon as the rope was secured around her chest, she lost her grip and slid down the face of the cliff.

Jeff grabbed the rope to keep her from falling further. With her help, he managed to pull her up next to him. He tied the excess rope between them to the main rope going up to the tree. This way, he wouldn't have her weight hanging on him as they were pulled up. "Mitch," he bellowed, his chest aching from the effort.

"Yeah, bro." Mitch sounded as though he was standing right on the edge of the abyss.

He probably tied the rope off. I hope he tied it good. "We're ready to come up. I'll help as much as I can, but you'll have to do most of the work from up there."

"You got it. Hang on. I'll get the others to help. We'll have you up in a jiffy."

"Macy, watch me and do exactly what I do." Pushing himself away from the wall with his arms, he lifted his legs and planted his feet against the wall.

Macy pushed off and lifted her legs, too.

"Okay, now stand up."

Pushing, they stood up, letting the rope hold their upper body weight as they stood on the face of the cliff. Macy's legs shook and Jeff feared she wouldn't be able to walk her way to the top. If she couldn't make it, he'd have to drag her up behind him. He felt the rope start to pull tighter. "Okay, Macy, here we go. Just go one step at a time and walk your way up."

She nodded and took a shaky step, her sprained ankle slowing her progress.

"Good, you're doing great," Jeff told her as she took another step. "Keep going, just like that. Before you know it, we'll be back on top." He put his right arm across her back to help her stabilize

She remained silent, but kept her feet moving. Sweat dripped from her forehead. Her face scrunched with each movement.

"How ya doin'?" Wayne called from above.

"Fine," Jeff said. He wondered why Wayne wasn't helping pull them up, but it hurt too much to talk. Nearing the top, he saw that Wayne *was* helping. He stood about five feet from the edge and pulled on the rope.

As Jeff's feet crested the top, he surged forward. Both Jeff and Macy collapsed on the ground at Wayne's feet.

Macy's pent up fear manifested in a torrent of tears.

Rushing to Macy's side, Mitch held and comforted her

while Carlita knelt down next to Jeff. Her voice rang with admiration. "Not bad, Jeff. Not bad at all."

"Thanks," he replied as he slumped back onto the dirt.

Riley approached with his computer tucked protectively under his arm. His pale face appeared scared to death. His usual self-confident, cocky attitude seemed buried under the cloak of fear. "As soon as you're up to it," he said quietly, "we need to go. I'm ready to get back to the clearing and go home."

Jeff sat up. This trip had been more dangerous than anything any of them had ever done in their lives. He was ready to go home, too. Loosening the rope from his chest, he pulled it over his head and threw it on the ground.

Mitch was already coiling it from the other end.

Carlita helped Macy remove her rope.

"How ya doin'?" Jeff said, kneeling next to Macy. "I didn't hurt you too bad, did I?"

Tears still streamed down her face. "I'm fine. You did what you needed to do in order to save me." She threw her arms around his neck and hugged him tightly. "Thank you for coming after me."

He held her close, proud of his actions and sensing a deeper connection to Macy. Even though he had always thought of her as naïve and slow-witted, they now shared a special bond and he would never look at her the same way again.

A strong aftershock suddenly shook the ground.

Macy buried her head against Jeff's chest and sobbed, while the rest of them rode it out.

CHAPTER 35

TERRY slowly came back to consciousness as the earth shook beneath him. As the tremor quieted, every bone in his body hurt. He felt like he'd been used as a human pinball.

He opened his eyes and looked around at the devastation that lay before him. He listened to the sounds of the jungle. All seemed quiet until a male voice came out of the silence from nearby.

"I think we need to get across this hole before it gets any bigger."

Terry rolled his aching body in the direction of the voice to hide behind a bush. As he slowly raised his head to see what was going on, he saw the group of kids standing near a wide, freshly formed chasm. One of the teenage boys helped the redhead to her feet. She seemed to be injured.

"I agree totally, dude," the blond-headed hunk said as he bent down in front of the injured girl. Tenderly, he said, "Climb on, Macy. I'll carry you across." He picked up the girl on his shoulder and marched after the others toward the fallen tree.

They're still here. Terry wanted to jump up and shout in elation. *And I'm still alive. I'm going to make it home*. His newborn hope and determination gave his body new strength.

As he watched the parade of kids make their way carefully over the fallen tree that crossed the chasm, he rose slowly and stumbled after them, keeping just far enough out of sight that they wouldn't notice him.

The earthquake had toppled trees here and there, causing enough damage to slow the group down by forcing them to take detours. This gave Terry a chance to stay up with them.

At this point, he would let nothing keep him from moving toward the clearing with them. All the way, he smiled evilly to himself, plotting how he would sneak up on them, shock them, grab the computer, and hit the button to return home. If that didn't work, at the worst, he would grab hold of them just as Riley flipped the button and make it back with the group.

AN hour later, Jeff staggered into the clearing where they'd started the day before. Some of the trees he had marked still stood, helping them make their way along their path. As it turned out, they didn't have to mark the trees. They followed the stream back. When he sighted Mitch's gun case, a sense of relief washed over him. Not wanting to stay another moment longer, Jeff turned to Riley and said, "Okay, get us out of here."

As everyone gathered around, Riley knelt down. He set his computer on the ground, inserted the backup battery, and turned the computer on.

Jeff gave a silent *thank you* at seeing the battery meter showing over three-quarters full.

Everyone else seemed to sigh in relief.

Riley adjusted his glasses. "As soon as I can, I'll pull up the time-travel program. Then, all I have to do is punch in some numbers and we can go home."

"How long will that take?" Carlita whispered, sounding out of breath.

Riley shrugged his shoulders. "Thirty seconds, maybe a minute."

"I don't think we have that long," she said, barely loud enough for Jeff to hear.

Quizzically, he looked at her.

She pointed to one edge of the clearing.

His body tensed. *Oh, crap, not again.*

A T-Rex stood behind the trees where Jeff had had his run-in with the Parasaurolophus the day before. He was sure the T-Rex hadn't been there when they'd come into the clearing. He wondered if it had been lying down to rest and stood up to investigate when it heard them.

As a low rumble resonated from the T-Rex's chest, everybody's eyes riveted on it.

TERRY came up behind a bush nearby the group when he heard a low growl. Looking up, he saw a T-Rex standing above the bushes just beyond him. It startled him into a frozen position. He wanted to run out into the clearing, expose himself, tell the kids that he wanted to go home with them, but instead, he stood terrified and numb, unable to move.

JEFF swallowed hard as his eyes stared at the monster.

"I'm hurrying guys," Riley said, his fingers flying across the keyboard.

The T-Rex bellowed and charged.

Huddled together tightly so they were all touching, Jeff could only hope Riley could transport them out of this moment in time before the T-Rex reached them.

The clicking of the keyboard buttons seemed surprisingly loud. Jeff feared it would be the last thing he'd ever hear.

Only ten feet away now, the T-Rex came storming toward them.

Jeff closed his eyes. He didn't want to watch.

"*Yes!*" Riley yelled with a jolt of his body.

Jeff felt an odd, tingling sensation flow through him. It felt so good, he didn't want it to end. Sensing they had escaped the hungry T-Rex, he kept his eyes closed and took a deep breath, hoping to prolong the wonderful feelings of the moment.

Suddenly, a strange, hostile-sounding male voice barked, "Who the hell are all of you?"

Macy screamed.

TERRY remained frozen as the terrifying T-Rex stumbled around, stunned and disoriented after the flashing bright light and the disappearance of his prey. It finally wandered off in the opposite direction.

Terry's heart sank at the thought he was now left in this frightening world with all these scary, man-eating animals. All the aches and pains in his weak, hurting body overwhelmed him. He plopped down under the bush and passed out from sheer exhaustion and hopelessness.

CHAPTER 36

JEFF opened his eyes at Macy's scream. He saw a purple man, wearing a shiny silver jumpsuit that looked like something from the future. With no hair on his head, not even eyebrows, the man's pink eyes stood out against his purple skin. But that wasn't the weirdest part. He stood on what looked like a silver piece of metal that hovered about a foot above the cement floor.

The man leaned forward and shot toward them, the metal plate under his feet glowing brightly as he moved. "Who are you and why are you in my house?" the man asked again as he swooped in close to Riley and snatched the computer out of his hands. Before any of them could react, he hovered on the other side of the room.

"Give us back the computer," Mitch growled. He pointed the muzzle of his rifle at the man.

"Oh, please," the man sneered without fear. "As if an old-fashioned firearm is going to scare me."

Is he mentally unstable or what? Jeff wondered. *Who wouldn't be worried having a gun aimed at him?* Maybe the man knew Mitch wouldn't shoot. Maybe he thought, as long as he had the computer, he'd be safe.

Suddenly, the man disappeared.

"Yoo-hoo, over here," came the voice from behind Jeff.

Jeff and his group spun as one.

The purple man now hovered in an open doorway. "I want you to stay here while I investigate this…this…" He held up the computer. "This antique piece of computing history."

Before Jeff could blink, the man was gone. The door closed.

Jeff turned to look around the room. He'd been expecting to return to his dad's garage, and this definitely wasn't a garage. If this was his dad's garage, it had been changed beyond recognition. Huge T.V.-like screens formed the walls and ceiling. The screens flashed one, then hundreds of different channels, switching between them faster than his eye could see. One screen would contain a full-walled picture one instant, then display fifty different stations at once. In another blink, it showed a hundred stations. At times, one screen would display a full nature scene that looked so real, Jeff felt he was there.

Mitch seemed to notice the same thing. He walked to the screen and put his hand on it. "I've never seen a T.V. with such clarity. What I wouldn't give to have one of these baby's in my bedroom."

"Where are we?" Carlita asked, looking around fearfully.

Jeff said, "I thought we would end up in my garage." He turned to Riley. "What happened?"

A pained look came over Riley's face. "I honestly don't know. I must have put in the wrong year by mistake."

"So, what?" Jeff asked. "We're in the future?"

"I'd say about a hundred years, or more," Riley stated.

Jeff felt too exhausted and disoriented to get angry. He just wanted to go home and get some relief from the dangers of their travels. Now, it looked like that relief was being threatened again.

Macy, holding her injured arm against her chest, moved closer to Carlita as though for comfort. "At least, we won't be eaten by a dinosaur here."

"Maybe not," Carlita retorted, "but who knows what the world is like now? We might be in more danger here than we were in the past."

Wayne's eyes stood wide with wonder as his little body turned in circles. "Just think of everything we can learn about the future and take back with us. We could know what was going to happen–"

"*No*," Carlita said firmly. "We don't want to mess with the future. If you do, you might mess up the past, too."

Jeff couldn't see how knowing certain things about the

future could hurt anything. In fact, it would be kind of nice to know some things, like who was going to win the Super Bowl or the World Series. Or better yet, the winning numbers in the Mega Lottery.

"I agree with Wayne," Mitch said. "There's no harm in knowing the future. I don't think there's any way we can change the past. I don't believe time will let you."

Macy looked doubtful. "Knowing your future may not change your past, but if you know something bad is going to happen to you, you will change your life to avoid it and change the future. That would have an impact of some kind."

"None of that matters if we can't get my computer back," Riley blurted. "I can't believe I screwed up, again." He put his hands over his face to hide his tears of anger and frustration at getting them into another mess.

Carlita hurried to his side. "It was an accident. You were in a hurry to put in the numbers. Look on the bright side," she said, lifting his chin so she could see his eyes. "None of us got eaten by that T-Rex."

"If we have to be stuck in another time," Wayne said cheerfully, "I'd rather be stuck in the future. Think of all the cool games and stuff they must have."

"We do have cool games," a high-pitched voice said.

Their heads swiveled around the room, but no one seemed to be there.

"Who are you?" Wayne asked. "Where are you?"

"I'm Mindnet."

"Mindnet?" Riley asked, drying his eyes. "What's that?"

"Mindnet is what you used to refer to as the Internet. Only now, it is controlled and surfed with the mind, rather than with a computer like the one you had with you when you came here…to the future."

"So, you know we're from the past?" Mitch asked.

"Of course. I know everything about you, too. You are Mitch Arnoldson, age 17. You have a mole on your–"

"*That's* enough," Mitch called out. "Nobody here needs to know where my mole is."

Jeff snickered.

Macy and Carlita blushed.

With his hand on his hip, Mitch gave Macy an annoyed look. "Did you have to tell her about it?"

"Getting back to Mindnet," Riley said impatiently. "So are you a person, or are you the actual Net?"

"I am all those and more. I am everyone and everything. I am all-powerful and all-knowing. I am linked into every person and every animal on the planet. I control everything from the weather to the food you eat every day. Without me, humans would not survive."

Mitch whispered loudly, "Sounds kind of full of itself, doesn't it?"

"I am not *full*," the voice said. "I can never be full. If I need more room to store data, I create more room. I am a never-ending entity."

"So," Carlita said wistfully, "if humans were to disappear from the face of the earth, you would still carry on?"

"Yes."

"That's kind of scary," Jeff said, thinking that maybe this new world may not be all fun and games like Wayne wanted to believe.

"Oh, not at all," the voice replied. "I have stopped wars. I have eliminated hunger. I have gotten rid of disease and racial issues and shown mankind how to live in peace and harmony with each other."

"Sounds to me like you're a dictator," Carlita stated.

"Yeah," Wayne shot back, "what if we don't want to eat what you tell us to?"

"Why would you not want to eat my food?" the voice asked in a hurt tone. "It contains everything you need to be healthy. It is formulated for each person according to their age, height, and weight. You–"

"Speaking of food," Mitch interrupted, "I'm hungry. It's been like 250-million years since I've eaten."

"Very funny," Macy said.

"*Red alert. Red alert*," the voice said. "I analyzed your stomach contents and you've recently eaten red meat. We will need to pump you out and sterilize your intestines."

Jeff's mouth dropped open as he backed toward the door.

" COMPUTER," a voice blared from behind Jeff.

Jeff swung to see the little purple man in the doorway.

"Stop intimidating our guests," the man said. "They think you are serious." He glided toward the group on his metal floating board. "I'm sorry the computer acts that way. It likes to think it's more powerful than it really is. It doesn't get a chance to communicate with someone inexperienced like you very often to play mind games."

Riley's shoulders slumped. He looked devastated. "You mean it really isn't in total control of your world?"

"Not hardly." He handed Riley his computer, then rose to the ceiling where he slowly turned and looked down on them. "Now, I have a dilemma in that you are all from the past and time travel is strictly prohibited." He pointed to Riley's laptop. "That is a time machine and having one is forbidden."

Looking worried, Riley stepped forward and took charge. "It was a mistake. We weren't supposed to come here. I was in a hurry and put in the wrong date. We were supposed to go home…to our time."

"I guessed by your clothing and your…" He grimaced. "Your primitive weapons…that you were from around the first part of the Twenty-first Century.

"What? You've got something better than this?" Mitch asked, brandishing the rifle. Suddenly, Mitch was thrown on his back and the rifle floated up to the man.

"Mind control," he said as he studied the rifle without touching it. "We learned fifty years ago how to control things without touching them. It makes it easy to protect ourselves from someone…or something…if all you have to do is think about it."

The rifle floated back to Mitch, who turned red with embarrassment and anger. "You didn't have to knock me on my butt. You could have just told me about your power. I would have believed you."

The man laughed. "No, I don't think so. You come from a period when you think you know it all. You were arrogant.

You thought you had control of me and it got you in trouble. I could have hurt you, but I decided to be nice and just knock you down."

Wayne butted in, "Why are you purple?"

"It's a fashion statement. In your time people got tattoos and pierced their bodies. We color our skin and shave off all our hair."

"Is the color permanent?" Macy asked.

"Oh, no. Last week, I was the most marvelous shade of red you've ever seen."

"Riley," Carlita demanded, "get us out of here. I'm ready to go home." She stood close to Jeff and he put his arm around her.

Riley opened the computer and turned it on. While he waited for it to boot up, the group scooted closer together for the jump. Riley typed in his password, but nothing happened. He typed it in again with the same result. "I don't know what's wrong," he said, trying again. "It won't let me in."

The man floated down until he appeared directly in front of Riley. "I changed your password." He shot across the room, up the T.V. screen, and turned upside down on the ceiling. Floating upside down, he lowered his face just inches from Jeff's. "You see, I rarely get visitors. I want to spend time with you...get to know you. You have so much to tell me about your time."

Jeff leaned forward. "You should know everything there is to know about our time. It should be on your Mindnet."

"Oh, it is. But it is going to be fun learning about it from someone who has lived it firsthand." He rotated until he was upright again.

Carlita nudged Jeff in the ribs. "Jeff, do something,"

He couldn't think of anything. After all, he wasn't the computer whiz. "Riley, can you reprogram the computer to take your password?"

"I'll try." Riley sat on the floor, put the computer on his lap, and started punching keys like a madman.

"It won't do you any good," the man said with a laugh. "Despite my father's wishes, I majored in computer sciences in college. He could never figure out why I would want to study something so outdated and...well...old."

"My brother knows more about computers than anybody," Wayne bragged, his hands on his little hips. "If anybody can figure it out, he can."

The man smirked, seemingly confident that he was going to get his way. "I'll fix up the spare room. It will be crowded, but I'm sure you'll make do." He floated toward the door.

Mitch raised his rifle, pointed it at the man, and pulled the trigger.

Nothing happened.

The man laughed. "So typical of an early human. Clueless when it comes to the real world." He spun and shot forward until he was right in front of Mitch. "I can read minds, also. I knew you were going to try to shoot me, so I blocked the firing mechanism of your weapon. Don't try it again or I'll have to hurt you." He disappeared in the blink of an eye.

Jeff, like everyone else, stood speechless.

FOR the next hour, Riley worked on the computer without success while the others searched the room for a physical way out. The single door was locked. Jeff and Mitch tried to force it open, but every time they slammed into it and cracked it, the door fixed itself.

Jeff couldn't believe they'd come this far to get stuck at the mercy of a mentally imbalanced maniac. He sat down in frustration, imprisoned in a room with a joking Internet personality probably studying them.

Mindnet. Jeff suddenly had a thought. "Mindnet, are you there?"

"As a matter of fact, I am," Mindnet answered.

Jeff brightened. "You said you know everything about us, right?"

"Yes."

"Can you read minds, too?"

"Of course. How do you think I get my information."

"So, you could read the mind of the man who is holding

us hostage and get the password for Riley's computer from him."

"I don't need to. I already know it."

Everyone's head turned toward Jeff with a look of hope.

Jeff waited, thinking the computer would reveal the password, then realized the computer only answered questions that were asked. "So, what is it?"

"*Time Hackers*," Mindnet revealed easily.

"That's the name of the program," Riley blurted. His fingers flew over the keyboard. "*Yes*," he shouted, pumping a fist in the air. "It will only take me a few seconds to get us out of here."

"Good thinking, bro," Mitch said to Jeff as he gathered his stuff and stood with the others.

Jeff felt justly rewarded with the thought of everyone safely going home.

"Okay, everybody, I'm ready," Riley announced emphatically. "Make sure you're touching someone."

Jeff visually checked to see that everyone was touching. He didn't want anyone left behind.

"Okay, here we go," Riley said as the purple man suddenly popped into the room.

"*No*," the man screamed, his eyes wide at the realization he was losing his visitors.

Jeff shut his eyes and hoped against hope that the next thing he would see would be his dad's garage.

CHAPTER 37

JEFF'S heart sank when he heard Macy screaming. He feared to open his eyes to see where they'd ended up this time. When he realized Macy was not screaming in fear, but squealing in joy, he opened his eyes to the familiar sight of his dad's cluttered garage.

"*Yes, I did it*!" Riley yelled as he hugged Wayne. Together, they jumped up and down.

Jeff felt relieved his parents' car was still gone. He'd been half afraid Riley would pop them into the garage a day early or a day late, and Jeff would have to explain where they'd been. He didn't know how he would do that.

Carlita sat on the work bench next to Macy. "I'm glad to be home. I can't wait to take a shower and get into some clean clothes."

"Me, too," Macy agreed.

"First," Mitch interrupted, "we need to figure out how you're going to explain your injuries to your parents."

While Macy's twisted ankle could be blamed on a rock she'd inadvertently stepped on while she was running, her dislocated shoulder wouldn't be so easy to explain. Neither would the cuts and bruises on Carlita's face nor Jeff's injured ribs.

The group sat silent for a moment, looking at each other, each wondering what kind of story their parents would believe.

"I got it," Jeff said, snapping his fingers. "We'll tell them we went camping for the weekend and were fooling around at night, chasing each other in the dark. We got a little carried away."

"I don't know," Macy said doubtfully with a frown as she studied Carlita's bleeding cut across her forehead in the florescent lights of the garage.

"I need a mirror," Carlita said, heading into the house.

"Macy's right," Wayne blurted, "that might explain some of this, but not all of it."

"I agree," Mitch added, "but I don't know what else we could tell them. Is there any way you can hide your injuries from them until you're better?"

"I don't think that's' a good idea," Riley remarked. "I think they need to go to the hospital and get checked out. That cut on Carlita's head needs stitches and Macy's ankle might be broken."

"My ankle isn't broken," Macy said. "And I'll tell my mom Jeff and I were dancing and he yanked too hard on my arm, hurting my shoulder. As I fell, I twisted my ankle. She'll believe that. She believes almost anything I tell her."

Mitch shrugged, like that was okay with him.

"Okay," Riley asked, "but what about Jeff's ribs and Carlita's face?"

Jeff said, "Don't worry about my ribs. They are more bruised than anything. Mom never sees me without a shirt on anyway. In a week, I'll be good as new."

Carlita came back with a small, round hand mirror. Looking in it at herself, she said, "This isn't that bad. I can cover most of these bruises and welts with makeup. The gash is a different story. Maybe I'll tell my mom I hit my head on a door or something."

"You think that'll work?" Mitch asked.

"Sure, why not? She never pays that much attention to me anymore. She's too busy with her new boyfriend."

Jeff detected a little bitterness in her voice. He'd suspected she and her mom didn't get along all that well with the new relationship. "I guess that settles it, then," Jeff said. He still felt different about himself, like he'd been on a long journey with many lessons and had grown years in wisdom. He'd never appreciated his friends or his little brothers as much as he did at this moment.

He turned to Riley and Wayne. "Now that we're safely

back home, I feel like I can tell you this. Riley, I'm sorry I didn't believe you when you said you made a time machine. You really are the best computer nerd I know."

"Thanks, Jeff," Riley said, bowing his head and blushing at the compliment.

"Just do me a favor, okay?"

Riley's eyes widened as he looked up expectantly.

"Don't use your time machine anymore. I don't want to go through anything like this again, ever."

"Don't worry." He pushed up his glasses. "I'm done traveling through time…for a while anyway. Maybe in a few years, when I'm an adult, I'll try it again. But I won't go back that far in time. It was *way* too dangerous."

"You can say that again," Mitch agreed heartily.

Jeff turned to Wayne. "And Wayne, I'm sorry I yelled at you the other night. We were all scared and angry. I shouldn't have taken my anger out on you."

Wayne grabbed Jeff around the waist and gave him a big hug. "That's okay, bro. I forgive you."

Jeff hugged him back. "At least nobody died while we were back there."

"True story," Mitch said, hefting his backpack to his shoulder. "It's time to head for home and get cleaned up." He stopped at the door. "You want to play a video game later?"

Jeff laughed. "Sure, I'd love to." Spring break was just getting started.

EPILOGUE

TERRY slowly awoke. Every bone in his body throbbed. He kept his eyes closed, a sick feeling coming over him as he remembered that the kids had disappeared right before his eyes and left him behind.

Someone cleared his throat.

Terry's eyes flew open to see three men, dressed from head to toe in camouflage uniforms, sitting on the ground and watching him. A large backpack sat on the ground next to each of the men and a rifle lay across each of their legs.

"Well, it's about time you came around," one of the men said. He looked slightly Hispanic but spoke perfect English.

They looked like they were from his era. His mind whirled with a rash of thoughts: *Are they from the FBI? The CIA? DARPA? Did Jake Clemmons send them? Could Jake have known what I was up to?* "Who are you?" Terry's eyes darted around in fear. "How did you get here? Did you follow me?"

Another man, a big one, laughed. "From the moment you got here yesterday. And I've got to say, I've never been so impressed and so disappointed in one person in all my life."

"What do you mean?" Terry asked as his aching body sat up slowly. His fear started to drain away. If they had intended to kill him, they would have done it while he was out cold.

"You got guts," the big man said, "but you're a little short on common sense." He smiled. "I missed it when you came out of that shelter covered with spiders. It would have been the highlight of the trip."

"Can it, Osborne," the Hispanic man said sharply. He glanced at Terry. "We need to go. The kids have gone and we don't need to be here any longer." He stood up, followed by the other two men rising.

Terry looked up at them, trying to grasp the situation. "You mean you really followed me here and have been watching me all along? Why didn't I see you?" After he'd blurted out the words, he realized he hadn't seen a lot of things while he'd been here. Heck, it seemed like he'd spent half his time either unconscious or asleep.

The Hispanic man nodded to the other two, who stepped behind Terry and lifted him to his feet. "Watch his injuries. We don't want to make them worse."

"What are you going to do with me?" Terry asked, slightly frightened about what might come of his unauthorized access into Riley's computer.

"Mr. Clemmons wants to have a little talk with you," the Hispanic man said. "So does DARPA and the FBI. You might even go all the way to the President. You have a lot of explaining to do."

"Yeah," the third man replied. "You're in deep doo-doo."

For a moment, Terry felt an urge to run, but he knew he'd only make a fool of himself before he was tackled and shackled. He sensed that, as long as he cooperated, these men would treat him fairly. Otherwise, he would be man-handled into submission. He sighed with resignation. "Fine, let's go."

The big man pulled a computer from his backpack.

Terry knew that a long interrogation, trial, and prison sentence awaited him back home. His chances of ever making another time machine and finding the cure to his illness was forever doomed. He especially hated the thought of having to face all the people staring at him, questioning him, making a mockery of his disability, and taking away every privacy that brought him comfort. He desperately needed his privacy.

The big man finally said, "Okay, boss, we're ready to go."

The Hispanic man and the third man put their hands on the big man's shoulders. "Everybody ready?"

As the others stared at him expectantly, Terry placed his hand lightly on the man.

Just as the big man hit the button, Terry jerked his hand away. His laugh echoed across the jungle, but there were no humans to hear it…just dinosaurs.

They said it wouldn't
happen in his lifetime,
but it did.

On December 21, 2012, the Yellowstone super-volcano
erupts.
Everything within 50 miles is instantly vaporized.
150 miles to the East in Buffalo, Wyoming, Sam Jones is
watching the evening news when he's suddenly thrown
across the room by a violent earthquake that quickly reduces
the surrounding countryside to something resembling a war
zone.
Sam flees, intent on getting his wife and two teenage kids
to safety, but things go horribly wrong when his wife is shot
in Casper, Wyoming.
A feisty Wyoming woman, a country in turmoil, and bad
luck all conspire against Sam as he's
Escaping Yellowstone.

Look for this and other books
by Layne Walker at amazon.com

Unimaginable Wealth,
Unimaginable Beauty,
Unimaginable Danger.

When Donny Jamison discovers a portal to an alternate world, he quickly realizes the financial possibilities and enlists the help of his brother, Eric. They put together a team of ten other people and, with the aid of the other-world natives, set off on a quest to gather all the gold they can find. But problems soon arise. Donny has to contend with an angry native who thinks the portal and everyone who comes through it is evil. Donny finds a world that's more dangerous and unforgiving than he'd ever imagined. One of the members of his group gets drunk and is accused of killing a young native girl. Will Donny and his group die violent, horrible deaths at the hands of bloodthirsty natives? Or will they make it through the portal and back to their world and safety?

Exploring the desert to avoid family guests, Gavin Clark steps into an invisible web and finds himself caught in a world where time and space are compressed. Dinosaurs and other dangerous creatures of past eras roam parts of the land. Groups of Earth's people from the past, present, and future come together in a melting pot of humanity, thrown into a new world without the advantages of modern technology and the comforts of their former communities. People age at a very slow rate. No children are born. And more importantly, no one has found a way out. Will Gavin find the key to escaping this world to be home with his wife and children again? Journey with him through a maze of peculiar people, shocking circumstances, and unpredictable events as he sets on out a quest to find the answers to getting home.

Look for this and other books
by Layne Walker at amazon.com

Layne Walker lives in Lake Havasu City, AZ, where he enjoys exploring the desert, dancing, and writing. He began his writing career in the summer of 2010 when he was challenged to write his own novel after years of being an avid novel reader. Once the writing fever got hold of him, he found himself on the adventure of his own life, constantly filled with new ideas for more novels, more action, more fun, and more surprises yet to come. To find out more, visit his website at www.laynewalkerbooks.com.